FlyGirl

Syd Blue

Blue, Syd
Summary: A 16-year-old girl learns to fly an airplane and in the process becomes Pilot-In-Command of her life.
ISBN: 0615709710
ISBN-13: 978-0615709710

Cover designed by Marianne Lins at Linsgraphics.com.

FlyGirl logo ™

For my husband, more than the wind beneath my wings.
The sky and the sun, too.

Thanks for taking the journey with me,
and all the generosity of your wonderful soul.

ACKNOWLEDGMENTS

Many thanks to my readers with insightful feedback. Thank you to those who either edited or inspired me: magical Daniel Morello, editor extraordinaire Cathee Sandstrom, adventure writer Cathleen Calkins, storytellers Christie Walker Bos, Cindy Tocci, and Vanessa Finney, terrific reader Tim Lavrouhin, insightful Irene Carter and her daughter Sahara, teacher Leigh Anne Drake and her son Jordan Romero (I found my Everest), kind Diane Burkinshaw, awesome flight instructor/airline pilot Margaret Watt, thriller writer Karlene Petitt, speaker Capt. Kahn, Thou-Shalt-Not-Bore inventive entertainer Maurice Kanbar, my adventuresome brothers and my ever-giving, hard-working, tireless parents.

Thanks to Women in Aviation, the 99s, AOPA, Young Eagles and all the pilots who share their love of flying with others.
A portion of the proceeds from this book will go to organizations that help those with a passion to fly grow their wings.

For more info about how you can help, too, visit SydBlue.com.

CONTENTS

Preface

"Epic," Robbie said as he fought the hyper gravity while attempting to move his arms to the yoke of the two-seater airplane. "Check this out."

Jill released her grip of the control column and let him have the plane. The Cessna 150 had two U-shaped steering wheels, yokes, — one for the pilot on the left side and one for the co-pilot on the right. Robbie put the plane in a sharp dive and turn.

Jill fell against the side window. "I bet we're pulling five Gs."

"You can take it?" Robbie handed her a barf bag and rolled hard into another turn. His biceps were flexing as he pulled back on the yoke. He smiled when he caught her looking at them.

She threw the barf bag behind her. "'Course. G-pulling should be a sport, like disc-throwing or something."

The G-forces eased up as he leveled the wings and the roller-coaster feeling dwindled in her stomach. She looked out the window to her left at a man, the size of a bee, digging a hole in his backyard.

At one thousand feet above the desert town of Landers, she could see what people were doing in their fenced yards. A thrill shot through her as they whizzed over the scene beneath them, blitzing faster than 120 miles per hour. This was so awesome. Flying a plane. With the hottest guy in school! Wait till she told Nikka. There's no way she'd believe her. Jill wished she had a camera to immortalize this moment, only the best moment of her life.

Suddenly the engine started making weird noises. The propeller sputtered, and awful, explosive, choking noises got louder. Her throat tightened.

"Um," Robbie said, "do these gas gauges work?"

Jill looked at the two gauges that both read empty. She stifled a gasp.

"Cuz if they do," Robbie continued, "that's not so good."

Jill's stomach jumped out her throat. Gas! Mr. Frib flew the plane and didn't refill it. How dumb could she be? She forgot about gas! The engine was quitting. They were going down. Ain't nothing you can do when you're out of gas. Hello.

She had been in such a hurry and distracted by Robbie, she hadn't even thought about the most important thing. Jill looked down at the desert floor clipping by. Outside Yucca Valley now, cactus, rocks and sage brush spotted the dirt. She held the plane level as they sunk, helplessly.

The engine sputtered out and the prop stopped windmilling. This thing was a glider now.

She could probably glide it down but landing was tricky. Pelting the ground this fast required a clear spot to touch down. Most likely, they would crash into something. No open, flat strips of land were anywhere around them for miles.

They were screwed. Boulders and Joshua trees jutted up everywhere. The rolling hillsides were cracked into channels of erosion and gullies. If they hit one of those, they'd flip over. Hard.

"Robbie, I'm so sorry. I think we must have had a leak or something. The tanks were full." Yesterday, she almost added.

"You can land out here, right?"

"Yeah, sure." They were going to die. She was going to die at sixteen with Robbie Magnor next to her. She almost pulled Robbie into a kiss. This was her last chance. She was going to die without ever being kissed. There were no words for what kind of Loser with a capital "L" she was.

The ground coming up grabbed her attention. Sharp rocks rushed by, raking closer. In seconds, it was all going to be over. Cactus ripped past as Jill tried to pull up on the yoke, but the plane only sank more, stalling out. If she lived through the next second, it wasn't going to be pretty.

1 Lift vs. Gravity

In the kitchen, Jill Townsend slapped together sandwiches as her sisters climbed up on the stools. The open floor plan of their airy log cabin merged the living area, dining room and kitchen all into one large space with high ceilings. From the counter, Jill could see the urn on the mantel. One word was scratched into the blue ceramic: Stardust. If the ashy remains of Dad were supposed to be stardust, why did it feel like heavy mud weighing on her heart?

Jill looked at her sisters and tried to lighten up. "Here's your vitamin-enriched dry food," Jill said, "otherwise known as cereal." She poured crunchy flakes into two bowls. "Kelly, drink your milk, please." She added some to Kelly's bowl as well as her cup.

"I don't have to!" Kelly shot back. How could tiny seven year olds blast so much volume? Even Bre covered her ears and she was used to a deafening Kindergarten classroom.

"Yes, you do." Quickly, Jill gathered her light-brown shoulder-length hair in a ponytail to get it out of the way, and then wrapped the sandwiches in baggies. "Hurry up because we have to leave in a few minutes." She pushed Kelly's bowl closer to her. "And please, not another episode of Girls Gone Neanderthal." Jill prayed her sisters would give her a break. She thought she might lose it and yell at them if Kelly pushed her today.

Kelly used the paper towel roll to hit the bowl, sending it flying. "I don't wanna go to school!" she yelled at full volume.

Biting back her anger, Jill retrieved dry paper towels from the cupboard and wiped up Kelly's food art on the walls. "Yeah, you're right. I'm sure there's absolutely no reason you need to learn to read and write. Completely useless skills for your species. I'll drop you off at

Caveman Crafts and Crusades. They're teaching the fine art of clubbing today." Even though Kelly didn't know what she was saying, it helped Jill chill and deal.

Bre spit out a mouthful of grub and stared at it as only four year olds could — like it wasn't a mess but something interesting and perfectly normal. Maybe even a convenient plaything that had just magically appeared. Before Bre could stick her probing finger in it, Jill wiped up the guck and sponged off the ruffled bib of Bre's pink jumper.

With her long dark locks flaring behind her like a mane, Kelly kicked the cabinet with the wild anger of a horse resisting taming.

Withstanding the urge to kick back, Jill pushed a banana at her. "Hurry up and eat something, please. I don't want you to get hungry later."

"Don't want to! Don't want to!"

"You little Tasmanian Devil," Jill said as she tickled Kelly, who couldn't help giggling in spite of her best efforts to launch World War III. Jill rushed to the cupboards and stacked up a pile of packaged food items as she stuffed a food bar in her mouth.

Kelly remembered she was mad and stomped her red Mary Janes next to Jill, trying to block her path to the counter.

Jill picked her up and moved her out of the way. "I know you're an Amazon in training and that's great and all, but can't we just get to school on time? I have an English test in forty minutes." She loaded lunch bags as Kelly pouted behind her, kicking her once in a while as if she were flicking flies off her legs.

"Don't want to." The kicks came harder as Jill tried to capture her hair in a braid, but Kelly would have none of it. Jill understood that Kelly and Bre felt comfort in routines. Kelly liked her hair loose, often in knots, and wanted to wear her red Mary Janes every day. Bre wanted pigtails with pink ribbons and her pink jumper with the ruffled bib. Somehow it was something they could count on. One consistency in a mixed-up life.

"Don't want to." Kelly wouldn't let Jill ignore her, but Jill decided this wasn't the time to try again to explain the threat of foster care if they didn't keep it together. There wasn't enough time. "I hate to tell you this, but you can't get what you want," Jill said. "The sooner you accept that you have no control whatsoever over your life, the better." Jill stuffed a slice of bread in her mouth and mumbled, "Like me. See?" She smiled a doughy toothed smile.

"You're not my mom. Leave me alone!" Kelly ran out of the kitchen and into Mom's bedroom. Jill tore after her.

"Mom..." Kelly crept closer to the lump in bed. "Mom..."

Mom turned away and stared out into space, unblinking.

Kelly crawled into her bed, seeking comfort in the warmth. "Mom?" Her voice came out weak, making Jill's stomach turn over.

Mom rolled further away from her second born.

Quietly, Jill watched her sister inch closer to Mom. She grit her teeth and went after her.

"Mom said I didn't have to go." Kelly resisted Jill's hands with all her might, clutching a bedpost.

"Come on," Jill said. She dragged Kelly out of bed as Bre watched. Mom didn't move. "I can't be late again. Do you have any idea what they do to tardy high schoolers? Do you know what tar and feather means?"

Jill pulled the petulant Kelly into the hall. With one hand she shoved a brown lunch bag in Kelly's arms and with the other she put a jacket on Bre while heading for the door.

"Bye, Mom," Kelly called.

They waited for an answer that Jill knew wouldn't come. She hated the way her sisters' heads hung so low. She didn't know what she could do to lift them back up.

2 Dead Stick

Wearing a black hoodie, jeans and Vans, Jill was a practical dresser. She could be cute and run a 100-yard dash all in the same outfit. With a novel inside her algebra book, she tried to read it without being detected. Math class was about as useful as a granny in a stickup. Through the window she saw Robbie Magnor swagger across the courtyard. Her heartbeat picked up, telling her she was still alive. Robbie always did that to her, turning her insides upside down. She watched his every move as she pretended to listen to Mr. Michaels drone on about integers. Whatever, who needs math?

Robbie, now that's a subject she could sink her teeth into. His deep brown eyes shot out confidence as he looked around the courtyard, an escapee from third period. He wasn't even on the radar until this year. Somehow arriving for his senior year ready to be the cutest guy in school, Robbie had caught the attention of every girl at Big Bear High. Jill was just another one, drooling on the sidelines. Worst yet, she was a lowly sophomore. No chance a senior would go for a sophomore. But she could watch...

At the open end of the elongated rectangle courtyard, Robbie stooped to tie his shoe, leaning a foot on the old broken fountain with a bear statute. Nice view of his sculptured glutes. Jill bit her pencil. Robbie's head popped up and looked west. She looked in that direction, too. A plane was flying low, too low. Really low. Barely above the buildings and pine trees. And it was coming straight at Robbie.

Robbie ran and ducked behind B building, across the courtyard from the building Jill was in. She stood from her desk, mouth wide open, pencil dropping to the floor, but unable to speak.

Astonished, she watched an airplane, hardly big enough for one person, sink down into the courtyard and smack down with a crack on the walkway between the buildings. With brakes squealing, it tried to stop before the picnic tables at the far end of the grounds.

Jill felt a crowd gather around her, gaping at the sight out the window. The red and white plane crashed into the picnic tables and rammed to a stop. She heard Mr. Michaels on his cell calling 911. Jill watched Robbie dart toward the plane. She ran out of the classroom.

By the time she got to the crash, twenty people were already gathered around yelling. Under the wing, Mr. Kimju, the science teacher, and Robbie were pulling hard at the door trying fiercely to get it open. Ms. Mods, the principal, yelled at everyone to get away from the plane, saying something about it blowing up and calling for classes to line up in their assigned emergency procedures. Within seconds of the chaos, Jill darted her way toward the nose of the plane where the propeller was all bent up. Inside was a woman with blood all over her face. She was calmly flipping switches and holding her sleeve to her bleeding forehead. Before long, Mr. Michaels arrived with a crowbar. He cranked the door open and helped the woman out of the plane.

"I'm fine," the pilot said. She shook off the helping hands, stood and looked at the plane. Her dark short spiky hair was matted with blood on the left side, which had dripped down on her black turtleneck and jeans. She spit blood and snarled, "And that's why you don't fly planes that have been worked on by someone else." She looked at the transfixed crowd. "Always do your own work. Always do your own inspections." She looked at Ms. Mods and demanded, "Where's the bathroom?"

"I'll show you," Ms. Mods said.

As they were walking off, the pilot looked back at the plane, saw Mr. Michaels looking inside it and raced back. "What are you doing?" she demanded.

"I… I'm… Is everything off? Explosion—"

"It's fine. It's not going to explode. Just a rough landing, is all." She leaned into his face, "And don't you dare call this a 'crash.' Just a rough landing, is all." She marched off to the bathroom faster than Ms. Mods could keep up with in her wool calf-length skirt.

As the teachers corralled the students back inside the classrooms, Jill hid behind the lockers. Robbie was hanging back, talking to Mr. Michaels. She strained to hear them.

"Finders keepers," Robbie said. "We could fly this for CAP."

"You know how much a new prop costs?" Mr. Michaels pointed

to the bent up propeller. "Fifteen thousand dollars. Civil Air Patrol can't even afford the tax on that."

"Cripes," Robbie said. "That's more than my car. What's it made of — Gold?" He carefully touched around the ripped edges of the steel blades.

Hearing sirens, Jill crept around the lockers and hugged the wall as she inched closer to the plane, hoping no one would notice her with all the commotion the firetrucks made. Two teachers met up with the arriving firefighters as the sirens died down.

"What do you think happened?" Robbie asked as he and Mr. Michaels looked inside the cockpit, around the seat and at the control column.

"There's obviously something wrong with this plane," Mr. Michaels said. "Rough landing? Yeah, I've seen plenty of rough landings when I was teaching students to fly, but they've always been at an airport. And guess what? You can fly the plane again after a so-called rough landing." Mr. Michaels looked down at the floorboards of the plane. Jill drifted away from the wall and stood behind the tail, hiding behind the vertical stabilizer.

"Crash or not," Robbie said, "any woman who can fly this thing is sexy."

Jill's ears perked up. She peered around the tail and saw Robbie move the seat to look behind it, at the back part of the cockpit.

"Don't touch anything," Mr. Michaels said. "There's always an investigation. We have to leave it the way it is, but I can tell you right now what the problem is." Mr. Michaels pointed to the cords running down to the pedals underneath the instrument panel, which had way more gauges than the dashboard of a car. "The cables came loose. She didn't have any control. It's amazing she landed. This bird is completely crippled. Even the throttle cable gave out."

"Hey," the pilot stormed across the walkway, "get away from there." Her face was cleaned up and she had a bandage on her forehead. Her short hair was still matted, which made it look even more spiky, but she didn't look hardly fazed by her little "rough landing." She banged the door closed on the plane and stood in front of it like she was guarding it.

"The cables came loose," Mr. Michaels said.

"No, really?" the pilot sneered and then launched into a tirade. "This isn't my plane. I was test flying it for a friend. It just came out of repairs, done by monkeys, obviously. Fourteen years I've been flying and this junker gets me. I'll never trust another mechanic again. No one puts care into their work nowadays. If you want something done right, you have to do it yourself."

Mr. Michaels stepped back. "Are you alright?"

"I'm fine," she shuttered and then took a deep breath. "I'm just mad. Sorry. I don't need an investigation. The FAA could suspend my license, and I can't afford that. I make my living flying."

"You do?" Robbie asked. "That's awesome. You're so lucky."

The pilot scowled at him.

"I mean, you're lucky to get to fly."

"Yeah, well, today my luck ran out." She walked over to a picnic bench that wasn't chopped up into a million pieces and sunk down on the table. Mr. Michaels and Robbie followed her. "I can't afford to lose my job."

Jill looked toward the firefighters who were still talking to Ms. Mods. A paramedic was walking their way with a blanket. A police officer followed. Jill looked for somewhere close by to hide. She slipped inside the cockpit and crouched down in the seat, peeking over the huge instrument panel.

The paramedic tried to put the blanket over the pilot, but she grabbed it from him and sat on it. He took out his blood pressure cuff and tried to put it around her arm.

"I'm fine," she snapped as she pulled away.

He stood back. The police officer slid out a notebook. "What's your name, ma'am?"

Jill peered over the instrument panel and out the cracked windshield at the crowd of teachers and firefighters. She would be so busted if anyone saw her in here, but she felt compelled to hear what was going on. She couldn't help herself. It wasn't everyday someone crashed landed at her school.

The cop took a step closer to the pilot. "What's your name, ma'am?"

The pilot looked at the faces all around her and swallowed. "Jane Doe?"

The cop widened his stance and stared her down.

She sighed. "Claire Cabello. But the plane belongs to Brian Hobsetter. And I want a full investigation of the monkeys who attached those cables. Someone's going to owe me loss of income if the FAA takes my license. You got that?" Claire's tough face nearly defused into tears. She fought them back. "I've been flying fourteen years without…" She got up and stormed off toward the bathrooms again.

The officer looked toward Jill's direction. Jill crouched in the seat.

She heard footsteps coming toward her.

Jill panicked. There was nowhere for her to go. She scrunched down further and closed her eyes.

"Hey," the cop said and opened the door. "What are you doing in here?"

Jill opened her eyes and smiled with a cringe. "I… I'm… I was just wondering what a plane… what it felt like to sit in a plane is all."

"Get out," he barked. "This is a federal investigation site. You are contaminating evidence."

Jill quickly slithered out, jumping down without using the step that was attached to the wheel beneath the wing. She nearly fell to the ground but managed to check herself.

"Get back to class," the cop ordered.

She sped back to math, tripping over her own feet. She hoped Robbie wasn't watching. She craned her neck around. At her fast pace, she lost balance and fell into the bushes. She looked at the crowds and didn't see Robbie. No one but teachers, paramedics, firefighters and cops saw her tumble. Only a dozen people, that's all.

She crawled out of the bushes and walked to class, now knowing what she would be doing next Saturday.

3 Thrust and Drag

"Eat the berries and I'll tell you," Nikka Judsudeson said as she stuffed a spoonful in her mouth between doing leg lifts with ankle weights, her dangly beaded earrings jingling in time. She pushed the bowl of granola, berries and fruit she had cut up toward Jill.

"Berries are for fairies," Jill said. "Tell me. What happened? I saw you talking to Cesar after fifth period. Don't deny it. What'd he want?"

Friday night slumber parties were a tradition with Jill and the only friend who had stuck around after doomsday: good ol' loyal Nikka. The two of them watched movies without the sound as they did leg lifts and ate the midnight snack Nikka had prepared. Since Nikka didn't approve of TV, Jill kept it muted, a compromise that had worked since sixth grade, the year Nikka deemed TV demeaning and repugnant. Nikka hooked up her satellite-radio receiver to the stereo and turned up the volume. Since the doomsday of Dad's death, the slumber parties were always at Jill's house. After she put her sisters to bed, she got her life back until sleep demanded its timeshare.

Jill swerved around Nikka, who was dancing to the music, in front of the couch. She turned it down — if her sisters were woken, there'd be no peace. Nikka edged the dial up a little. Whenever Sirius XM wasn't on, which was never, she was still dancing to a beat in her head. Since satellite radio didn't have commercials evilly trying to persuade people to make purchases, Nikka approved of it as a source of fresh tracks. Dancing was Nikka's favorite exercise, hands down. She lifted her knees to the beat as she chewed on a carrot.

Jill stuffed a celery stick into her mouth. "Nikka, we eat all the time and then have to work it off. Wouldn't it be easier to just not eat?"

"Girls who don't eat are weak." Nikka took a big bite of raw broccoli. "You can't run away from homicidal maniacs when you're starving. Anorexic Annie's too puny to run ten feet. It's totally healthier to eat like a horse and run like one too."

"Horse? Great," Jill said. "Thanks for the analogy. I love being compared to a large solid-hoofed grass-eating beast of burden. Now you've totally lost me." But she bit into a slimy green thing anyway. "You are such a freak. You know you're tired of fruits and nuts." She kicked her. "Come on, admit it. Even someone as loony as you."

"I'm the greatest source of amusement in our small town, donuts-are-a-pastry life and you know it." Lounging onto the floor, Nikka tinkled the little bells on her skirt. She always wore long, natural-fiber skirts. In the winter, she wore pants under her bohemian drapings, but she was definitely a skirt girl. Even when she exercised. It was more convenient that way since she was always moving. She inherited beautiful tan skin from her Malaysian father and honey golden hair from her Finnish mother. Even now, doing leg lifts, she was undeterred from the skirtage, but Nikka was never one for doing things the easy way.

"You're so nutty the squirrels try to carry you off to their holes," Jill said.

"I've told you a ba-zillion times, you develop a taste for natural foods. You've never given it a chance."

"I did once when I was a very small fairy, eating flowers in the woods. Now, that I'm five feet tall—" She stood up and beat her chest. "—Big strong human now. I like hamburgers. Umm, cow flesh."

"Cow farts destroy the ozone. Girl, I love you but you've got to get off it."

Jill sighed at their old arguments. She depended on their friendship too much to care about their differences. When everyone at school thought Dad's death was contagious or something, Nikka was there making jokes about Dead Daddy. It wasn't disrespectful. Jill could almost feel Dad laughing at the jokes, like how they put some of Dad's ashes into pickling jars for Uncle Bryan and Grandma Liz: Dad To Go. He would have loved that.

Jill looked at the Stardust urn on the mantel, which held what was left of Dad's remains after distributing him throughout the family. There was plenty of him to go around out of the big package from the mortuary. Flesh and bones of a whole human don't whittle down to just a cup, more like a bag of planting soil. A sack of gray ash and white bits of bone. And she knew Dad would want to be spread all around since he always wanted to travel. With Dad in To-Go jars, it was like he could finally see the world with Grandma Liz in Toronto, Uncle Bryan in Florida and all the others who wanted a piece of him. Thank God Nikka had found the humor in the logistics of mortality when she was helping Jill package him up. Mom let them do it, but she couldn't witness it. Nikka, less than half Mom's age, was the one who got Jill through wrapping up the details of death. She had a natural wisdom about these things that was clearly lacking in this household.

Jill saw what Nikka had set up in the dining area and wondered how long she could avoid it. She wasn't ready to dive into a project like that yet, so she flew up and raided the kitchen. She heated up and snarfed a leftover hamburger patty. Nikka didn't want to let the cow thing go. "Go ahead; clog your arteries. Methane up the planet."

"I will." Jill took a big bite. "Clogging commenced." Juice ran down her chin as she watched Nikka punish her hamstrings.

Nikka switched sides for her reps. "I have a date tomorrow night."

The hamburger hit Jill's stomach like a rock. "No way," she said. "Not fair. I still haven't even kissed a guy and you're going out on another date. What is that? Like three this year? You have to save some of the town for me."

"We're actually going down the mountain to a Jam an hour away. Cesar thinks he can teach me a *Dirty Dancing* move or two."

"You? He obviously hasn't seen you on the dance floor. You're so ouch, ouch, hot. I wish I could go." Finished with her snack, Jill wiped her fingers on a dishtowel and launched onto the floor to continue her exercises.

Nikka flipped on her back and lifted her arms and legs in the air. She looked like a fallen rollie pollie that couldn't get up. "Why don't you ask Robbie out?"

"Me? Ask a senior to take me, a mere sophomore, out? You're dreaming."

"You've only been pining for him since the dawn of time. You're worse than the effeminate poets of the nineteenth century who thought unrequited love was tragically beautiful." Nikka threw a pillow at her. "Lame. Ya gotta get that boy before he graduates."

"I'm working on it. We've actually progressed a lot in our

relationship. You'd be so proud. We've gotten up to a—," Jill lowered her voice seductively, "'Hey.'"

"Impressive. Should I start writing the announcements, ordering the catering and picking a religion for your minister, since you're moving so fast and all?"

Jill threw the pillow back at her, hard. "I do have a plan, though."

"What?" Nikka used the pillow for leverage on another callisthenic.

"Can't tell you. You'll try to stop me." When Jill could take no more leg lifts, she stood up and grabbed a paintbrush from one of the easels Nikka had set up for them in the dining area of the room. Newspapers laid in wait underneath to catch the excess of creativity. Jill held a tube of red paint and then changed her mind and picked up blue. It was time to tackle their art projects.

"What's your plan? Tell me."

Jill ignored her. "Why is blood blue before it comes out of you?" She looked at the veins in her hand. She mixed colors on a palate until she was satisfied the color matched her veins. "I can't help wondering what he looked like... when... you know... I can't get the image out of my head, what his face looked like... with blood..."

Nikka held still for a change.

"Don't stop," Jill said. "It makes me feel worse when you stop."

Nikka flinched her hips to the beat of the new song playing. She turned it up. Jill lowered the volume again, looking toward the hall to make sure her sisters weren't awoken.

"It's been one year," Jill said. "Today is his death-a-sary."

"Necessary to honor the death-a-sary," Nikka sympathized.

"Life goes on." Jill swiped blue across her canvas.

"Maybe it's because of the way he died — that it's so hard to go on." Nikka tilted her head as she studied the white canvas on her easel. "It's not right to die that way. That would mess up anyone."

"When someone drops dead," Jill continued, "you have a million questions. I want answers."

"I thought you just wanted a boyfriend before you're seventeen." Nikka smiled, easing Jill back into a simpler subject.

"It's not my fault I live in a small town. Finding a decent guy is like trying to find tofu on a fast-food menu — and he doesn't even know I'm alive." Jill put her paintbrush down. "Maybe there's something wrong with me." Jill frowned deeply. "Am I, like, the only one in high school who hasn't had a boyfriend?"

"Joe hasn't."

"I mean, even you've had a boyfriend."

"Thanks a lot," Nikka said. She threw her slightly wavy hair behind her shoulders and stared harder at her canvas. "No big. We just wanted guaranteed dates to the school dances. It's a matter of convenience. There's nowhere else to go dancing around here. Thus a relationship is born. It's not my fault Vince broke it off because he couldn't handle my style." Blending her unique range of dance moves, Nikka demonstrated with a CrissCross Botagofo, Running Man and plié. Jill swayed a bit to the music but wouldn't dare try Nikka's moves.

"You scare everyone," Jill said. "No one in our Hallmark Channel, conservative community knows how to deal with a girl who refuses to conform to the standards of polyester and leather. Luckily, I'm here to be your BFF. Keep you out of the Sheriff's Log." Jill picked up some newspaper and waved it at her. "I'm so glad they report every loud disturbance in town. Here—" She read from the paper. "Last week 'rock music' was reported coming from the two hundred block of The Boulevard. Oh, and somebody broke into the shoe repair store."

"News you need to know."

Jill returned the paper under her painting since it was dripping. As she bent over to pick up another paintbrush, her ponytail dipped in the blue paint. She decided the pigment complemented her brown hair and left it. She watched Nikka stare at her blank canvas as her shoulder ticked to the beat of the music.

"Why don't you paint a vegetable?" Jill asked. "*Portrait of Okra in Green Number Five.* I have a stake in this, you see. We have a bet going in class on how weird yours will be." Jill wished she could feel as good about being different as Nikka did. Nikka was famous for her eccentricity. The year of her dreadlocks was only topped by the following year when she shaved them all off, completely bald.

"But you know," Nikka said, "weird pays off. No one buys real art from posers." Nikka looked at a painting on the wall that her mom had made for Jill's mom years ago. It was an impressionist vision of people being struck by rainbow lightning.

She looked back at her blank canvas. "This is so lame. It's oxymoronic that an art class doesn't let you decide what you want to paint. I don't want to do a self-portrait. Art can't be dictated. Artists are the freest beings there are."

"Next to pilots," Jill said. "Flying looks pretty awesome. Maybe that's why Robbie wants to fly. I could learn."

"Wouldn't you be afraid?"

"If my dad could die doing something people do every day, then nothing's safe, so who cares?" Jill refocused on her canvas. "I like the assignment." Jill dabbed another roll of paint on her palate, a rich cobalt blue. Maybe she'd show her class who she was in her painting, and they'd actually stand up and clap.

What a dreamer.

Nikka read her face, the daydream, and laughed, kicked her. "Standing ovations?"

"I'd settle for a passing grade."

Nikka cocked her bobbing head at her canvas as if trying to get it to cough up secret insights. "The problem is once you lay down one brush stroke of one color, everything's changed. Your possibilities are limited after that. When it's blank, you could be anything."

"Yeah, blank!" Jill said. "Boring!" Jill's painting was now a thick mixture of various shades of blues, in swirls, lines, zigzags, and something that looked like bird wings. "This is good." Jill stood back and admired her painting.

Nikka peered over at her bestfriend's creation. "Feeling blue?"

"Black and blue. Why are you supposed to wear black out of respect for the dead? How do they know dead people like black? Some things about life I don't get."

"Like how dumb people can be? Did you hear that Robbie nearly took out eight people yesterday? He accidentally drove up on the sidewalk as he was turning the corner. Too fast, as usual."

"See, that's what I mean. His canvas already has a color: fast."

"I think his color is clueless." Nikka danced off to the bathroom. "He should totally have noticed a hottie like you by now."

"He will," Jill said when Nikka was out of hearing range. Jill was determined to get Robbie's attention even though no one that cute could like her. She was no model. She was decent looking, but not perfect. No high cheekbones, no tiny button nose and no balloon lips. Luckily, she wouldn't have to make a living through her looks. Actresses and models did, and yet somehow women in every profession thought they had to match them on their prime employment features.

Nikka returned from the bathroom. "This is your last chance to make it happen. Robbie's graduating in, like, three months."

Jill sighed. "I'm going to bed. I'm tired." She closed up the tubes of paint and wiped her brush off.

"Don't forget about tomorrow. I'm counting on you being there." Nikka swiped one red line across the canvas and then quit. "I can't do it without you. Promise you won't forget?"

"I promise. But I win major bestfriend Brownie points for this. I'd rather eat large hairy spiders on a stupid reality TV show than go to another one of your things," Jill teased.

"That's what bestfriends are for."

"I knew there was a reason to skip signing up for best-friendship. Having someone to talk to about anything is highly overrated. They make 900 numbers for that now. Madame Clara is such a good listener. And for three dollars more a minute she'll tell you you're about to meet someone new, in a place you always go, sometime in the future."

"Just be there," Nikka sighed.

4 Angle of Attack

With mostly sunny skies, Saturday was a perfect day to do what she was about to do. She had to hurry if she was going to make it back in time to keep her promise to Nikka. Jill nearly fell off her bike, twisting her neck to look behind her at the bald eagle circling above. Jagged-tipped wings stretched out and soared the currents with just a small flex, a flutter, to stoke it faster. Effortless flying.

Searching the sky, Jill's sienna brown eyes found the faded mustard Cessna she was looking for, hovering near the north mountain ridge. She pumped the pedals harder, trying to get to the airport before the plane, the size of a dragonfly at this distance, landed. As it swooped down, the plane entered the landing pattern, an invisible box in the sky above the airport. A flock of airplanes in line were already ahead of it, taking turns to land. Since the Young Eagles were giving out free demonstration flights today, the traffic was extra heavy, even though the day was almost over. Jill knew about Young Eagles but had never been interested until Robbie was drooling over the pilot who crashed at school, Claire Cabello.

Jill hopped off her bike when she reached the chain-link fence of the airfield perimeter. She didn't see Claire's plane in the sky. She hoped she wasn't too late. She hoofed her bike along to the center of the west end, where she could see the full length of the runway.

Though the February air was nippy, Jill sucked it in like it was candy. She loved it here. Since there weren't trees or tall buildings around the airport, it was a good place to see the sky, full wide. The runway left a wide patch of clear open space, a mile west to east. The hangars bordering the north and south sides of the runway always seemed to bustle with happy people parking their planes or rummaging around their hangars, preparing for a trip to the coast or Palm Springs for lunch.

On this snowless and unseasonably warm day, everyone who owned a plane was out enjoying it, friendly to the other pilots because they belonged in the club, Those Who Know No Limits. Above it all.

She guessed that's why they always smiled at her when she walked on the airfield, pretending she belonged there, maybe walking to a relative's hangar. She had pretended so many times that no one questioned her presence. It wasn't hard to slip through the lobby when the clerk had her head down in paperwork, monitoring the radio to hear what the pilots were saying to each other and ready to provide information if someone asked. At a non-controlled airport, pilots didn't need permission to land, just respect for others coming and going. And the clerk had seen her many times saying goodbye to Dad when he left on a quick commuter flight for Los Angeles.

Jill clutched the fence and wished she knew what the lights and windsocks on the runway were communicating to the pilots. A Mooney airplane, with a tail like a half boomerang bending frontward, rolled down the runway toward her. The plane lifted off and flew straight over Jill's head. She nearly screamed with the rush of the roar busting away as the plane gained altitude fiercely. Turning around, she watched the plane head over the lake. As a van sputtered on the road that separated the airport from the lake, it blocked her view, along with a long line of fuming cars, and she lost sight of the plane.

Big Bear Lake, a small town in the middle of a mountaintop valley, was surrounded by ridges going up to eight thousand feet on both the north and south sides. On the shores of the lake were mansions, vacation homes of the wealthy and rentals for the Los Angeles tourists who were looking for a winter wonderland. But it looked like winter was going to skip this year. The only snow in sight was the man-made stuff at the ski slopes.

Straight on, she caught sight of Claire's mustard-colored plane coming in to land. In seconds, it was only a few feet over Jill's head as it aimed to set down on the white lines marking this end of the runway. The plane was heading in the opposite track of the previous traffic. Jill saw the windsock had changed directions. She had seen Claire's Cessna many times at the airport but didn't really take notice of it or Claire until the day she "landed" at her school. The plane touched down with a *chirp chirp* of the tires and rolled away. Jill rushed to the corner of the fence and around to the front of the airport. She locked her bike to a rack in the parking lot and hurried inside the lobby.

She waded through the pack of thirty kids and strained against the rope that herded them behind a glass door. Above them was a "Young Eagles" sign. It was always crowded on the days the Young Eagles were giving free rides.

Beyond the bobbing heads, Jill could see Claire pull her Cessna 150 into a tie-down spot behind the lobby. She casually worked her way through the crowd, past the ropes and out the door. She waited for the propeller to die out and then rushed to the plane, nearly bowling over the reporter heading to interview the ten-year-old who exited from the passenger side. Jill looked back and saw the boy smiling broadly as he spoke to the reporter.

At the front of her plane, Claire took a screwdriver to the cowling over the engine. Jill walked up and stood by the door expectantly.

"You think the old bird's gonna make it?" Claire asked.

"Well, it hasn't fallen out of the sky yet," Jill said. "You must have a good mechanic." She watched her unscrew a little door on the nose of the plane. Jill reached up and grabbed the wings and looked inside the cockpit, smaller than a Miata, except for the twenty feet of wings. The two narrow seats left very little space for luggage. But who needed baggage?

Claire wiped her hands on her no-nonsense attire: jeans and a T-shirt. She opened the cowling and slid out the oil dipstick. Turning it in the sunlight, she inspected the honey color and level and slid it back in. "Wouldn't you rather go for a ride in that new Bonanza?" Claire motioned to a sparkling bright yellow airplane with a split tail, surrounded by three kids. The pilot helped each one climb the low wings and crawl inside.

"No way." Jill touched the pole going from the wing to the landing gear. "Yours has more character."

"That's one way to put it." Claire adjusted a bolt on a silver hoop around a hose in the engine.

"Let's go." Jill pulled on her Roxy hoodie. "Burning daylight. We'll never make it to the Caymans before sunset at this rate. How far can this thing go anyway?"

"We'll be staying in the valley. I don't know how I got talked into this. With gas seven dollars a gallon, I only go flyin' when a client is payin'." She wiped grease off her hands and closed the cowling on the engine.

"It's your humanitarian duty." Jill smiled.

"Good one," Claire said. "That's what I should have told the reporter." Claire seriously needed some good PR after her little incident at the high school. Rumor had it that Claire was once an airline pilot but no one knew why she wasn't now. No one knew what had happened to her career or why she was a pilot in this small town, which wasn't exactly the pinnacle of aerial transport.

Jill opened the door on the right, the copilot's side. "This is my first flight." She could feel the excitement beaming out of her, like rays of sunshine.

On the other side, Claire reached in the cockpit and grabbed a coffee mug. She slurped down all its contents, then tossed it behind the seat. "Your parents didn't want to see your first flight?" Claire threw on a baseball cap.

"My mom doesn't get out much. It's her goal in life to become agoraphobic." Jill climbed up on the step above the wheel and launched her leg inside the cockpit. "It's going to take more than me breaking gravity to get that woman on her feet. A trip to the moon, that might do it." Jill almost let the heartache launch her into an exposé. In truth, she'd love to tell Claire all that had happened in the past year, but she didn't want to scare her away. Claire was her one chance for flight lessons. If the only woman pilot in town didn't take pity on her, fat chance anyone else would give her free instruction. If Robbie thought girl pilots were sexy, then hot diggity, she was going to become a pilot.

The metal headliner near the door bumped off Claire's cap when she got in. There was much less space in the cockpit than the front seat of a car. Two seats in front side by side and a small baggage area behind barely fit two average-sized people and a backpack. The instrument panel took up a whale-sized chunk of space. Forty instruments surrounded two U-shaped control columns, which were the steering wheels for the wings. Jill turned the control column in front of her and the one in front of Claire moved in exactly the same way.

"Dual controls," Claire said. "How 'bout if you don't touch anything."

"It seems you and your plane have a very exclusive relationship."

"Yes and it's very high maintenance." Claire sprayed some WD-40 into the squeaking door jamb before she shut the door. "Ten thousand hours working jobs I hated to get the money to buy my own plane and all I could afford was this old thing."

"Umm, she'll stay in the sky, right?" Jill rubbed a finger in a worn groove of the door handle. Maybe Claire's old bird wasn't the ticket after all.

"This wasn't my idea. You can still back out." Claire set the altimeter. "I've flown her twenty hours a week, every week, for the past four years with no incidents in this baby. You do the math."

Jill almost said something about how she wasn't good at math, but decided to cool it. She was ready to get going. She had to see what it was like — flying — up close and personal, to see why Robbie envied flying and why Dad always returned from business trips with a huge grin on his face that didn't fade for days. He loved it when his company let him take a commuter ride to out-of-town meetings. He was like a kid when the pilots would let him sit in the cockpit, pulling knobs and turning dials. It hurt to remember, so she grabbed at her seatbelt.

Fumbling, she tried to figure out how to fit together the four pieces of the belt and shoulder harness. Three loops and a hook somehow fit together. If she didn't get it figured out pretty soon, Claire might leave her behind for her lameness. She was failing at the simple task of belting up. Oh brother.

Claire grabbed her own belt's shoulder harness and slid the puzzle pieces together, adjusting it taut. Jill copied her.

"Pull hard," Claire said. "You need it as tight as possible in case we hit turbulence. The weather gal said it might get bumpy today out over the north mountains. Those cumulus look friendly but—"

"Friendly cumulus?" Jill asked. "And I thought I needed to get out more."

"You got that right. Last time I had a day off was 1912." Claire pushed a red knob all the way in, flat against the instrument panel. "Anyway, we'll try to stay out of the choppy air. Cumulus clouds indicate lots of chop."

Jill regarded the sky. It looked good to her, even though cloudbanks had moved into the vicinity. So, clouds meant something was going on there with the air currents, huh? Cool. A visual giveaway to bad air.

Claire yelled out the window, "Clear!" She started up the engine and the propeller suddenly whipped to life. As it did, it became invisible. Jill closed the window because the prop blew in loud, forceful wind.

Claire gave Jill a headset and plugged it into the instrument panel.

"Can you hear me?" Claire asked into her mike. Even though the mike was right up against Claire's mouth, it still let in some of the scream of the engine, but Jill could hear her fine in the thickly padded earphones, wrapped like supersized doughnuts around her ears.

"Good to go." Jill shoved her ponytail behind her shoulders to watch Claire perform her preflight checklist. She turned the control column and watched how the ailerons moved on the wings. She pushed the control column all the way in and all the way out. Jill turned behind them and saw the elevators, the little wings on the tail, move in response to Claire pushing and pulling the control column in and out.

"How much gas do we have?" Jill asked as she looked at the round dial above her head, attached to the wing. The needle was bouncing between empty and half a tank.

"Why? You buying? This thing guzzles fifty bucks an hour. Flying takes some deep pockets."

"Unfortunately, my pockets are as deep as an Oompa Loompa's." Jill wished she had some money to give her. Her family wasn't exactly in a position to be generous. "All I'm saying is you can't pull over to the side of the road if we run out, you know."

"There you go. That's thinking. Now, you're smarter than all the idiots who run out of gas and crash into someone's house. See, you'll make a better pilot than them."

Jill smiled.

Claire let the plane roll forward and taxied it to the runway. "Don't worry. We have enough gas for all the flying we're gonna do today. I could fly to Vegas on this tank." Claire patted the gas gauge above her head, connected to the left wing. "Okay. Final check. How's the oil pressure looking?"

Jill found the oil pressure gauge and played along like she knew what was going on. "Good to go." Good guess, since the needle was pointing to a green arc on an instrument labeled "Oil." Even Homer Simpson could get that one.

Claire adjusted the propeller faster and the plane shook. "You ready, FlyGirl?" Claire asked. Her mood seemed to swing upward with the rush of the prop and the frenzy of the wind it was creating.

Jill nodded vigorously. She loved nicknames. FlyGirl. Cool.

Claire pushed a button on the control column and spoke into her mike in an official tone. "Big Bear Lake traffic, Cessna Two Five Whiskey, departing runway two six, Big Bear Lake."

The button broadcast her voice on a frequency used by their hometown airport. Jill wondered how many car accidents could be avoided if drivers had some way like this to communicate to each other.

Claire rolled out onto the runway. "Let there be flight." She pushed forward the throttle and adjusted the gas-to-air mixture. As she eased up on the pedals, the plane rushed forward.

With her feet, Claire steered the plane down the runway. It charged down the strip, picking up speed and banging with the rip-roaring wind. When their speed reached fifty miles per hour, she pulled back on the control column and the plane's nose lifted up so much that Jill couldn't see over it anymore. She looked out the side window to see the horizon.

Quickly the world fell far below them. The airport buildings shrank to bricks. The streets and buildings looked like her sister's Lego playset, square structures blotting the landscape. All around the basin, trees popped out of the earth no bigger than furry toothpicks. The cars raced around like insects, their purpose no more meaningful than ants.' In the center of the valley, the seven miles of lake shimmered like a blue puddle as the mountain ridges were reduced to anthills. She smiled as Claire leveled off the plane.

"Goodbye, land-locked losers," Jill said. "Hello, endless sky." She looked at Claire and thought she saw a faint smile.

They circled the valley, flying around one of Southern California's few national forests. The view topside was awesome — superior. More distance could be covered, and Jill could even see the high desert beyond the mountains. It seemed to stretch on forever, an expanse of freedom, not just miles of road hindered by stop signs. This was an ever-changing sphere of possibilities. She thought she could see the curve of the planet, with so much to explore, not just by looking below, but the sky was another world all its own to investigate laterally, vertically. There were two worlds up there: the spacious sky and the busy ground.

As they turned above the lake, Jill saw the road she lived on, which wound behind the row of houses hugging the shoreline. She saw the secrets her neighbors shoved in their backyards — treehouses, swing sets, broken trampolines, moldy Jacuzzis, and horses in their pens.

On her street, she saw her neighbor, the size of a beetle,

sunbathing in his backyard, totally unaware that he was being spied on.

As the plane flew lower, Jill liked that she could watch people who didn't even know there were eyes peering down at them. It was like being part of the world but not really. An observer, not a participant. An angel. Moving faster than those bound to gravity. Gliding rather than grumbling over the surface. She suddenly understood freedom from the world — from limits, rules, and boundaries. Not following a road or path. Emancipation. And more than that, she could see where all the paths went. She had always felt she could see the big picture and now it was literally true. The world seemed so much bigger, yet smaller at the same time. And it looked different at various altitudes. One thousand feet above the ground was more detailed than two thousand feet, but the higher they went, the more the sky became a world of its own, contoured by cloudscapes.

Claire rolled the plane into a tight turn as she pulled the nose up to gain altitude. Jill's stomach flopped. She liked the feeling. It was the best roller-coaster she had been on. Surrounded by windows, there was nothing like flying in a small plane, with hardly anything between her and the sky. Up above the shrinking world, the vast expanse of the sky took over. This gorgeous infinity could set her free from anything. She hadn't felt this good for more than a year. Actually, she wasn't sure she had ever felt this good. It was like she was truly alive for the first time.

Then, Jill noticed something strange. And it was straight ahead of them.

5 Pitch, Yaw and Roll

Directly ahead, a lone cloud the shape of a mushroom cap floated in their path. The plane banked and turned toward the mountains, avoiding the rotor cloud.

Claire pointed to the wings, with deflected ailerons, and then to the attitude indicator. "You don't want this to show that you're turning more than forty-five degrees."

"Yes, that would be bad." Since Claire didn't respond to her joke — she was all business — Jill concentrated on the view outside.

Suddenly, it got quiet. The roar of the engine became a softer buzz. What happened to the engine? The nose pitched down.

"Did you put the engine on mute?" Jill asked.

"Oh man!" Claire yelled. "The engine's gone out!"

Jill felt her eyes bug out the size of baseballs. "What's happening?" Okay, so maybe flying wasn't as good as she thought.

"We're gonna crash and die!" Claire cried.

Jill's heart stopped. She had chosen the wrong plane. Her heart started beating again double time, flooding her with adrenaline. Jill tried to think what her last prayer would be, but her mind went blank. She squeezed her eyes closed for a moment. When she opened them, she saw Claire thrust a knob back in and the engine kicked back up. The plane resumed forward flight. Claire snickered.

"That's screwed up." Jill punched her softly in the shoulder.

"Just wanted to see if you'd keep your head."

"There's something seriously wrong with you."

"Yeah and you're trapped up here at ten thousand feet with me."

"Unfunny." But it was kinda … thrilling. As her heart rate returned to normal, she felt more alert than before. She was more grateful for that spinning thing making so much noise on the nose of the plane.

"You gotta admit, it makes the flight more interesting," Claire said. "You should have seen the trickster who taught me to fly. Gotta be prepared for anything up here. The number one reason pilots don't make it out of emergency situations is freezing up. They stop flying the plane. A lot of pilots who get themselves in trouble end up crashing because they're so busy berating themselves for a bonehead mistake that they can't concentrate on dealing with the situation. It's good to learn to keep your head — then you can get yourself out of nearly anything. Flying is not for the faint of heart. Takes some guts and a whole lot of head." Claire pointed to her brain. "It's not for everyone."

Jill wondered if it were for her. She wasn't really a thrill seeker. She didn't go bungee jumping with Nikka, even though Nikka had paid for her. She didn't ski or snowboard because it was too fast. And flying was scary. Nothing under them but wind. Thousands of feet in the air. But she loved it. She did. It was the very definition of freedom.

Claire took the plane higher, and Jill tried to look over the monstrous nose out the windshield.

"You can look at these to see where we're going." Claire pointed to the navigation instruments. "I always keep one eye looking out the window for other planes and one eye on the instruments."

"No wonder you look a little cross-eyed." Jill looked at Claire to see if she'd react. Claire Cabello was back to stone-faced shale, absorbed in the instrument panel. Jill followed her gaze. Jumping needles displayed speed — they were going 110 miles per hour! — oil pressure and other engine functions, demanding attention. Way, way more than a car dashboard or anything else for that matter.

"What's that?" Jill asked.

"That's the attitude indicator," Claire said.

"Altitude?"

"No, that's here." Claire pointed to a something that looked like a clock face, except the number five was in the six o'clock position and a zero was at the top. "The altimeter displays the altitude we're at, but the attitude indicator tells me if I'm level to the ground, so I don't fly into it."

Its gyroscope had a miniature airplane pointed above the horizon line. Jill looked out at the mountains and confirmed that they were in a climb.

"Attitude indicator? Where's the 'needs improvement' label?"

"In my case," Claire yawned, "it would be 'needs coffee.' You ready to turn back yet?"

Jill quickly tried to divert Claire's attention so they could stay up longer. She didn't ever want to go back down. "I've actually read about these gyroscopes, kaleidoscopes and periscopes. I'm totally down on the phenomenon of flying. Did you know that the youngest pilot in the world was a seven-year-old girl?"

"She wasn't a licensed pilot and her flight instructor had constant control," Claire said.

"I can fly." Jill tried to take over the control column, but she couldn't get it to turn. She looked to her left and saw the resistance was coming from Claire's vice grip on her side's control column. She wasn't letting go.

"Yeah?" Claire said. "What's a stall?"

"A stall is when the plane loses lift," Jill said. "When the plane is pointed up too much, the wind breaks up over the wings and there's no more lift happening. The plane falls out of the sky. Without lift, you're toast."

"Pretty good. Do you know how to break a stall?"

"Pray?"

"Put the nose down, level the wings, and goose the power in, full throttle. Faster speeds stop stalls if you mind your angle of attack."

Jill yanked the control column to the left. This time, Claire let her. Jill was digging the range of motion.

"Now keep your nose down until it shows you're level." Claire pointed to an instrument.

Involuntarily, Jill lowered her own nose as she pushed the control column forward to lower the nose of the plane. She hoped Claire didn't notice.

"There ya go," Claire said. "You're flying."

Jill couldn't suppress the smile taking over her face. Piloting the plane was even more fun than flying as a passenger. She felt the control, even with small movements. A push down on the yoke and the horizon changed. She stomped on a rudder pedal and the plane yawed to the left.

Suddenly, the plane started jumping around. The control column bounced underneath Jill's hands.

"It's okay," Claire said. "It's only turbulence." But Claire took over the control wheel on her side again.

They bumped around a bit, jumping several feet downward in a downdraft and then instantly popping up higher with an updraft, like they were a plaything for invisible forces. Jill became even more aware of the lack of anything solid beneath them. She grabbed her seat and held on.

All of a sudden, the clipboard in Claire's lap flew up with a wind shear and banged against the instrument panel. "Yep," Claire said. "A bit bumpy today. Let's try it higher." She pulled up and flew the plane to a higher altitude.

Out the window, clouds were appearing. The closer they got, the more the clouds dissipated into mist, insubstantial puffs. They only looked thick and billowy when viewed from a distance. Up close, they looked like they were alive, stretching out their tendrils of mist, reaching for them.

Jill opened her jaw and wiggled it from side to side. "My ears hurt," she said. "I think my head's going to explode."

"I'll get you some gum," Claire said. "It helps relieve the air pressure." She reached into the back for her dufflebag and retrieved a piece of gum.

When Claire looked back at the GPS, she found that they had gotten off course and they were completely surrounded by white. Claire pulled on the control column to try to clear the cloud, but the wisps seemed to be following them.

"Clouds are dangerous when you're flying VFR because a plane could be headed straight for you and you'd never see it coming."

"What's VFR? Very Fun Rotoring?"

A shock of turbulence sharply banged the plane around.

"Make sure your seatbelt is tight," Claire said. She reached to tighten her own seatbelt just as an eddy of air hit. In a jolt, her hand accidentally unlatched her buckle. *Click.* She was free floating in the ups and downs. Another jerk and Claire's head banged hard into the metal headliner.

She hunched in her seat. Jill swallowed her gum as she looked at the lump in the seat next to her.

"Claire?" Jill tried to rouse her with a nudge.

Claire's eyes were closed and she wasn't responding. She was knocked out.

"Claire!" Jill shook her. Claire's knees were pushing the control wheel out, toward them. The plane's nose headed up too much and the airspeed dropped until it seemed like the plane was crawling along.

Chopping noises startled Jill. The stalling air broke up over the wings and caused the plane to bang around violently. The stall alarm shrieked, nearly stopping Jill's heart. Then, the turbulence banked the plane sharply sixty degrees to the left — they were almost completely sideways!

An instrument display showed in the red. Suddenly, the nose dropped. And Jill couldn't even make sense of the altimeter, which seemed like it was winding down.

Claire's head fell against the now down-facing window. Jill was trying to lean against the turn, to up-right herself, but the force of accelerating gravity sat on her lap like a refrigerator and pulled her head around like a rag doll.

"Claire!" she screamed. "Help!" Her first flight and this terror? Was this going to be her last flight? Her last day on Earth? Who would take care of her sisters? She wished she could hug them now. She wanted out of this thing.

Everything turned dark. Pelting sounds ripped into the windshield — it was rain bulleting the plane.

The wings bounced back to horizontal, but they seemed to be floating backwards, with the front of the plane rising up more and more. Jill panicked at the surreal sensation. She looked at the fuel gauge over her head and saw the needle dropping. Should she switch tanks? The stall alarm kept shrieking. Jill wanted to scream back at it. It was the scariest sound she ever heard.

The plane bounced wildly — one second the wings were almost vertical and about to roll over on its back and the next they were horizontal again. In the fury of the clouds and wind, the plane was like a Ping-Pong ball.

Suddenly, the plane dove downward, going faster and faster, exiting the cloudy soup. The rain drove fiercely into the windshield as the ground was coming up fast.

"Help!" Jill screamed, utterly helpless. She clenched the yoke so hard her hands hurt.

Jill had to do something to keep the plane from diving into the thickly treed hillside.

6 Full Throttle

For several long tense moments, her hand skirted across the controls trying to recall everything she had learned.

The plane dropped like a rock. The wind whistled like a mad tea kettle.

Confused, Jill adjusted knobs, trying anything. She grabbed at her control column, pulling up the nose sharply. The plane was now pointed too high, but she was scared to edge it down at all, since she didn't know how close the ground was beneath them. They had re-entered the mist and it could be hiding a mountain ridge.

Again, the plane stalled. The stall alarm shrieked. The wind banged against the wings, rocking them savagely. The plane slowed down so much it seemed to stop.

Like it was dead in the water, no longer flying, it floated into stalled madness. They started to fall out of the sky. It seemed like they were drifting out of control for an eternity.

She forced a big breath in, and then, it came to her, in a flash. "Faster speeds stop stalls," Jill recited. "Full throttle." She pushed the black knob all the way in. She pushed the nose down to the horizon and corrected the banking, returning them to straight and level flight. Clearing the cloud, bright sunny sky greeted them.

The plane flew smoothly again as Jill controlled the wheel column, reacting to every pull to keep them level.

Claire came to. She looked around and saw that Jill was flying the plane and everything was fine.

"What happened?" Claire rubbed the side of her head.

"So that's why you don't take off your seatbelt during turbulence," Jill said.

Claire looked casual, unaware of any trouble, like nothing had happened. "So, how's it going?" She asked as she relatched her seatbelt.

Jill shook her head, exasperated, yet she was pleased with herself. She was in command of the plane. "You got knocked out. You were totally dozing."

"What?"

"We went into a stall!" Jill said.

"Hmm," Claire made a skeptical sound, but after she checked all the instruments, a deep frown set into her face. She adjusted the throttle. "That's all I need." Angrily, she rubbed her head.

"I have everything under control." Jill moved the yoke like a pro, maintaining level flight. "I can handle it."

"Let's go home," Claire said. "Newer planes don't have exposed metal headliners." Claire punched the bar above her. "This old thing is out to get me. All I need."

"Which way is home?" Jill looked down, but she was disoriented and couldn't make out the streets and buildings. It wasn't as easy to make out the landmarks when she had lost her point of reference. She had no idea where the airport was or what direction to head. What did pilots do when they couldn't find an airport? Jill strained to look harder at the terrain and make sense of the labyrinth of roads.

Claire pointed to the left.

Jill turned the yoke and the plane banked hard to the left.

"Easy there, FlyGirl. Don't want to pull too many Gs." Claire took the control column in hand, but the only thing Jill let go of was a relieved laugh.

"You should have seen us a minute ago. I like pulling Gs." They battled for the yoke. Jill wouldn't let go.

"Haven't had enough, huh?" Claire asked.

"I can do it," Jill said. After what she had just been through, she felt like she could do anything. She didn't want anyone taking this feeling away.

Claire let go. "Keep it lined up here." She pointed. "That-a-way." She switched the fuel tanks setting. "I was the same way when I got my hands on a plane. It ruined me for boring office jobs."

"Oh, darn, I was hoping to preserve my aptitude for boring office jobs. My life is over." Jill glanced at Claire. Still no laugh. Talk about a hard nut to crack.

"If you like it so much, you should learn to fly," Claire said.

"I thought I was," Jill smirked.

"Wait until the landing. That's the hardest part. It takes much practice."

In no time, the plane was descending toward the runway. Claire cranked the flaps and took over the control column.

Jill started to feel anxious. "Practice? And you've had some?"

Claire smirked. "Watch this." She slowed the throttle and set down more flaps. "The flaps increase the wing surface and help us stay flying at lower speeds."

Jill noticed the little pine trees out the window growing to normal size. As they approached the runway, a crosswind blew them about. "Easy now," Claire coaxed the plane, applying some rudder and getting them back into line with the runway in front of them. Over the runway, when the downdrafts made the wing dip, Jill thought the low wing was going to smack the ground, but Claire reacted perfectly to the movements, like she was gracefully ballroom dancing with the wind. Claire's face lifted as she maneuvered the plane.

"What's the second most thrilling thing known to humankind?" Claire recited the old pilot's adage with a spark in her eye.

"Flying."

"What's the first most thrilling thing known to humankind?"

"Landing." It was a corny saying, but now she understood completely. Landing was by far the trickiest part.

Jill absorbed Claire's every move, but it all seemed to be happening too fast. Between the seats, there was a circular dial that Claire kept trimming, as she called it. She cranked a lever and the flaps on the wings extended down another nick. She adjusted the gas mixture and the carburetor heat and several other things Jill couldn't keep up with. Her heart sped up as she anticipated meeting the quickly approaching ground.

"A good flare eases the nose up without climbing," Claire said. They seemed to hover a few feet above the runway before Claire set the plane down. They gently sunk into the earth as if they were reattaching; the magical spell of flight was broken. Even though Jill could feel the bumping of the tires on asphalt, she wondered if they were down on the ground for good. But the plane didn't lift up again. It was true: Jill's mingling with the troposphere was over. They had completely rejoined Earth.

The tires bumped them along toward Claire's hangar. Jill lifted her feet off the floor of the plane because the ground felt rough beneath her, lurching into every bump in the road. Maybe flying was for people who weren't so grounded.

They taxied past the Young Eagles action near the lobby. Jill noticed the reporter was gone and the line of kids had dissipated some.

Claire kept the plane moving toward the rows of hangars at the northeast corner of the airfield. She maneuvered to a spot in front of her hangar at the far end corner and parked it there. Jill had seen Claire's hangar before — no room for an airplane.

"It's over?" Jill asked.

Claire got out and tied rope anchored from the ground to the wings. "All wheels firmly on the ground."

"That was so cool! When can I go again?" Jill was no expert but it was obvious that Claire was an amazing pilot. She handled the plane like it was an extension of her, with ease and self-assurance.

"Uh, wait a minute," Claire said. "I have a pretty busy schedule." She lodged wood blocks around the wheels. "I don't have time to keep giving free rides. See, when you're all grown up, they reward you with lots and lots of bills. I have a ton of bills—"

There went Jill's hope of pity lessons. "I'll pay." She wanted to add, I'll pay anything. I want your life, free as a bird.

"A hundred dollars an hour," Claire said as she looked at Jill, studying her expression. Jill nodded like it was no big.

"And you'll need permission."

"No prob. You mean, from my parental units, don't you? Easy." But Jill's face belied the impossibility of that. She hid her disappointment as much as she could as she watched Claire dart away into her hangar.

Easy.

As easy as Earth reversing course.

With the taste of flying in her blood now, Jill couldn't go back home and face being a land-only creature, a mere mortal. The feeling of soaring ripped through her veins, making her pump her bike as fast as she could, whizzing down hills trying to get that roller coaster sensation back in her stomach, if even for a fleeting moment.

As her bike took flight off ramps, her mind was speeding through ideas to get back in the air. Now that she had seen the world from a small plane, she couldn't accept her life the way it was. The wind had blown away the storms inside her and she felt more awake than ever before. It was like a chocoholic discovering Godiva. She couldn't go back to a generic life when she had taken her first breath in her real world.

She now knew where she belonged.

Up.

7 Approach and Departure

Even though it was freezing outside in the school courtyard, Jill took off her hoodie and sat on it. She shivered in her tank top. Nikka laughed at her as she danced around to keep warm, circling the benches by the broken fountain. Her reputation for Dancing Queen reached even those who didn't attend school dances. She had been known to demonstrate Touch Jam, like Twister to music, in the middle of the outdoor cafeteria at lunchtime. It amazed Jill how some people who ran around calling Nikka weird still became entranced by her moves, surrounding the scene as if she was a street performer in the city. The name callers were probably just jealous, anyway. Nikka could win any dance-off, any day.

Jill looked over at Robbie and his entourage, Coby, Trevor and Heath, skateboarding in the courtyard. She liked watching him move, a style of ease. Balanced and confident, he kick-flipped over a rail. She had to admire how sure of himself he was. If he had been a bird, he'd be a soaring eagle rather than a heavy flapping goose.

Heath ollied up onto a bench, yelling at Robbie. "I'm telling you, only morons crash. They take off too heavy and can't get the bird to fly. I heard that's what happened to Liam's dad. He had four people, a dog and snowboards crammed into his Piper Archer. Didn't make it over the first powerline. Tragic."

Straight on, Robbie slammed down from a jump and did a quick skid stop. "Yeah, I was working CAP when it happened. We were first on scene."

"And you still want to fly?" Heath asked.

"What?" Robbie sprung his board up into his hand. "'Only morons crash.'"

Jill tried to catch Robbie's eye by stretching. He looked in her direction but looked right through her.

"Sweet," Robbie said. "There's one on final now."

All the guys turned and looked in Jill's direction, but not at her. Above her head, an airplane was coming in for landing. Trevor grabbed his digicam from his backpack and turned it on, framing the horizon.

"Not again," Coby said. "It looks too low."

"There's a sink hole in the air right there," Robbie said, "two hundred feet from the end of the runway. Grabs suckers all the time."

"Power, Fool," Heath said as he grinded on a rail.

"He's got it." Robbie slid over on a bench next to Jill's and strained to look over the trees. "Lucky dog, I'd kill to fly."

"In your dreams." Heath hopped on his skateboard and launched over some stairs.

"Heat alert!" Coby said.

All the guys popped their skateboards up into their hands and tried to look innocent, holding them as they walked away.

Mr. Vandenholder, the social studies teacher, yelled across the courtyard, "You're not skating here, are you, boys?"

"Who us?" Heath pointed to his chest, looking indignant. "Of course not, Mr. Vandenholder. That's against school rules."

The guys disappeared behind Building B. Jill looked down disappointed.

"At least, now," Nikka said, "you know how to get Robbie's attention. All you need is a plane and a pilot's license," Nikka laughed.

"Is that all?" Jill slumped off the bench and headed to fifth period. There was no way she was going to tell Nikka that she was planning on doing just that.

8 Flare Out

Jill fed her sibs TV dinners in front of the glowing square babysitter, otherwise known as the TV. In her favorite pink jumper, Bre fussed like a baby over her hunk of meat until Jill cut it up for her, singing her a Sesame Street song to try to get her to quiet down. Bre's whining was shredding the last of Jill's nerves. Kelly nibbled hers without protest. She could subsist on sawdust as long as it was served on her Disney princess plate in her green Nantucket chair, which she kicked non-stop with her red Mary Janes.

When the TV had them mesmerized, Jill left them alone. She took some water to Mom in bed, who was surrounded by a shrine of litter — tissues, half-eaten Lean Cuisines, photos of Dad, medicine bottles and various other remnants of consumption.

"Mom…"

Mom stared out into space, unblinking. Jill sat on the bed next to the large lump and pet her arm, trying to rub life and love into her. Her brunette bob was tangled in a ratty mess and her night shirt was stained with a rainbow of colors resembling mustard, spaghetti sauce and a few things unidentifiable.

"I want to take flying lessons," Jill said. "Kay?"

"No," was all Mom said. Her eyes didn't move from whatever speck of space she was staring at.

Jill hated to see her like this. This horizontal daze had gone on for way too long. She wanted to shake her out of it, light a fire under her bed or something. Nothing else had worked.

"I want to become a pilot," Jill said. "I can start lessons now and get my license when I'm seventeen."

"No," Mom said, in between her long, slow breaths. The act of breathing was all the work she could handle.

"Gee, I'm so glad you're willing to talk about this." Jill waited. "Please, Mom…" Jill threw away tissues as she waited for some response, then decided to try a different approach. Mom used to respond to logic and statistics. "You know, flying is safer than driving. There're one-tenth the accidents. There're only twenty-five mid-air collisions a year. That's way less than driving, where there's a one in a hundred odd of dying in a car accident. Forty thousand Americans are killed a year in cars!" She cleaned up spilled mashed potatoes from the side of the night table. "In fact, no one should ever drive again. We should all take helicopters to school."

Jill grasped Mom's slack wrist and checked her pulse. "Hey, it may be permanently horizontal, but it's alive. It's alive!" Jill said Igorish. "It's alive!"

Not even a crack of a smile crossed Mom's face. Jill dropped her arm and stood in front of her. "Listen, you're allowed to fly alone when you're sixteen, so I'm already behind on practicing solo, Mom. If it's legal, it must be safe. You know, just like—" Jill picked up a prescription bottle and read from it. "Diazepam. Good thing the doc gave these to you. They're working so well."

"I said no and that's it."

Jill looked at her hopelessly and then at the photo of Dad. She opened her mouth, ready to tell Mom what only she knew, what Dad had told her in confidence. But she was afraid the revelation would make Mom sink even lower. She closed her mouth. She was really tempted, though…

Jill huffed down on the bed and purposely jostled around. Maybe Mom just needed to be stirred. "When I get my pilot's license, I can fly you to Nana's. Wouldn't you like that?"

The rise and fall of Mom's chest was the only clue she was still on Planet Earth.

"Come on," Jill pleaded. "I'll give up TV for the rest of my life. That's how much I want to fly. That's way more than Frodo wanted The Ring."

"Your sisters need you." She sniffed. "You're a better mother than I am. After what I did…"

"What are you talking about? How could you possibly blame yourself? You're losing your mind." She decided to keep Dad's secret to herself.

"You don't know…" Mom buried her face in the pillow.

"Come on, Mommy. Get up." Jill heard her sisters scream at each other in the living room. "Please get up," Jill said softly as she kissed Mom's dirty hair and left to referee the twosome.

As she tore her sisters apart and held the only one who would let her, Baby Bre, she felt her spirit sink. Knowing now what made her heart soar only caused her to be more aware of how bad she felt, grounded here. She couldn't go back to the zoo after exploring the jungle. She watched a blue jay out the window, winging around the patio. She was a penguin with stumps that could not fly. What an ironic misfortune of nature. Why have wings you can't use? That cruel question echoed in her empty chest and burned her. Why have wings you can't use?

"It's bedtime," Jill announced. Kelly ran under the dining table and locked her arms around a thick wooden leg. When she took this stance, there wasn't any way Jill could muscle her into pajamas. It was pointless to fight against this coup d'etat, but Jill tried anyway.

"It's time for bed and I'm afraid there's nothing you can do about it, Kelly-Belly," Jill reasoned. "You can't do what you want. That's not how life works. So, might as well get over it."

"Yeah, get over it," Bre mimicked. Jill patted her head gently. She knew nothing about raising children, and her honest approach wasn't working. Honest in that she was telling Kelly like it was. Wasn't it better to prepare Kelly for life than to let her get disappointed? She'd do anything to spare her sister from what she felt

Jill heard a plane fly overhead and sighed. When she looked back at General Custer and her last stand against bedtime, she was staring at the urn. She knew Kelly's ache, but what was she supposed to do?

"I'll tell you a bedtime story," Jill offered. "Do you know the story of Amelia Earhart? She was the first woman to fly an airplane across the Atlantic Ocean. Do you want to hear about her?"

Kelly didn't answer but she left her post and sat on Jill's lap next to Bre.

"They call her a pioneer in flying because she opened up the skies for women. She did what no woman had done before so that we can become pilots."

"I want to be a pilot," Bre said.

"Oh, but Baby Bre, you already have wings. I can see them

here." She touched Bre's back, pretending to pet feathers. "You must be an angel." Bre giggled.

"Am I an angel?" Kelly asked.

Jill cleared her throat. "Sure you are. You have magic sparkling dust in your hair. It must have fallen off your halo. Do you see it?" she asked Bre. Bre nodded as Jill stroked Kelly's hair. "I'm so lucky I have little angels for sisters."

"I thought I was a Taz-min Devil," Kelly said.

"What do you think you are?" Jill asked.

"Both." Kelly grinned.

9 Diamonds Are a Girl's Bestfriend

In the bright sunlight at the airport, Jill cupped her hand between the window and her forehead to try to see inside the plane. It was a gorgeous Diamond DA20 with low slender wings, a pointy slim tail and a canopy with so much window, the view of the world had to be all-encompassing.

Old Vern scuttled toward the plane with his ancient headset in his hand. The wires were taped up and the ear pads were losing their stuffing. Stooped over, Old Vern wore the same threadbare white shirt and blue windbreaker every day. He was sweet, but could he see good enough to fly? He looked like he was well over eighty. He saw Jill and opened the cockpit door.

He smiled, baring old graying teeth. "You're my two o'clock?" Old Vern took about three minutes to climb in the seat on the right side of the Diamond.

Jill watched him as he huffed and puffed.

"Well, get in," he said. "It's your dime. Every minute costs two dollars. Young people don't know the value of a dollar anymore."

Jill looked at the empty pilot's seat. She looked around the airfield. No one was around at the moment. Where was the student he was expecting? If it had been her lesson, she would have shown up early. That student obviously didn't deserve flight lessons. For about two seconds she considered how much trouble she'd get in if Mom found out she was even near an airplane, let alone taking a lesson. But Old Vern had been flying half the history of flight. What could go wrong? Mom would never find out and Jill would get to feel what it was like to sit in the pilot's seat, to control an airplane, just like a real student pilot. She jumped in.

Old Vern showed her how to start the plane. "Pump the throttle a few times."

Jill pushed the throttle all the way in and pulled it back out two times. The throttle was like the gas pedal in a car but instead it was a knob to her right on the instrument panel.

"Turn on the master switch and magnetos," he said.

Jill could figure that out since they were clearly labeled.

Then, he pointed to the start button. Jill pushed the start button and the propeller turned until it caught. It quickly became invisible. Between its loud racket and the wind it generated, Jill felt a rush of excitement stirring in her chest.

Old Vern demonstrated the pedals and told her to try the control column, which was a stick coming from the floor, just like a joystick, between her knees. She rotated it all around.

"Let's go. Turn to the left." He pointed the way out of the parking area.

Without thinking, Jill turned the stick in front of her. The plane kept going straight. Then she remembered the rudder pedals steer the plane on the ground. She stomped down on the left pedal and the plane whipped to the left.

"Settle down there, Missy. Apply some brakes to slow down."

Jill pushed at the top of the pedals with her toes. The plane veered to the right.

"Apply both the brakes evenly."

Jill concentrated on getting her feet to push against the pedals the same amount. She had to keep her feet off the floorboard to be able to manipulate the tops of the pedals. It was a workout to hold her legs in the air.

"Good. Follow the yellow line up to the runway entrance."

Jill tried to follow the yellow line but when the plane veered in one direction, she applied more pressure on the pedal in the opposite direction and the plane veered off that way. She wobbled back and forth all the way down the line until she reached the end of the taxiway. She didn't dare look at Old Vern to see if he was laughing at her or frustrated. When she got to the end of the pavement, she pushed both brakes hard and held them.

"I'll help you get around this tight corner onto the runway." His leathery hand helped guide hers on the throttle as they revved up to turn onto the runway. She could feel the left brake being depressed under her foot. Old Vern was using his set of brakes to round the plane sharply onto the end zone.

"Okay, whenever you're ready, Pilot," he said. "Push the throttle all the way in and release the brake pedals."

With his left hand on her right hand, she clocked the throttle all the way in to the panel faster than he could react and try to slow her hand. The engine howled. Soon the plane was racing down the runway.

"Pull back gently on the yoke."

Jill jerked it back with her left hand. It was so much more responsive than the last type of plane she was in. Suddenly, she felt resistance and pulled back harder on the handle. She saw Old Vern was holding the stick in front of himself and controlling the pitch. Just as soon as she wished he'd remove his hands and let her have it alone, he did. "You got it, Pilot. It's all yours," he said.

The nose of the plane veered left.

"Don't forget rudder for P-factor," he urged. He was talking about P-factor on takeoff. She had read about that. She applied right rudder to hold the nose straight.

The Diamond handled differently than Claire's plane. It seemed lighter and more sensitive to small movements of the control column, but after a few minutes, she was used to it.

Looking down at the streets below, she saw they were going faster than the cars and it thrilled her. Switching hands on the stick, she grabbed the armrest with her left hand and squeezed, afraid she would float out the window being so happy.

She glanced over at Old Vern. His eyes were closed. *Oh God, the old geez isn't asleep, is he?*

Old Vern's eyes popped open. "Now, climb to eight thousand."

Jill adjusted the control stick for a modest climb. She stole another glimpse at Old Vern. His eyes were closed again.

After a few moments, he opened his eyes to give another instruction. "Fly heading two nine zero and descend to three thousand five hundred after the mountain ridge," he said. She pretended to look away and caught him closing his eyes again. She sighed. As long as he was awake for the landing, she'd be fine. It wasn't very hard to fly around in wide open space.

Jill watched the altimeter until one hand was on three and the other was on five. Jill looked at Old Vern. His eyes snapped open. He nodded. "Continue," he said and closed his tired eyes.

"How many flight students have you had?" Jill tried to keep him awake with conversation.

Old Vern held his eyes at half-mast. "Oh, more than I can count. I've been doing this fifty-two years. More than 20,000 hours now…" He nodded into sleep. Oh well.

Jill loved looking at the landscape over the high desert. She loved spying on people's homes and scouting how they lived. She loved seeing where everything was and what was out in the world around her. After a while, though, Jill wondered when the lesson would begin. Weren't there things, like maneuvers, Old Vern was supposed to be teaching her? She looked at him and he was still napping. After a few more minutes, a voice came over the radio.

"Aircraft two miles into Restricted Area One-Five, identify yourself."

The voice repeated and somehow Jill had the feeling the voice was talking to them.

"Vern, I think they're talking to us. What should I do?"

Vern didn't answer. Jill looked at him. He was still sleeping like a baby. Whoever was paying for this lesson wasn't getting their money's worth.

"Vern, wake up."

Jill looked at him again and a terrible feeling came over her.

"No!" Jill shoved Vern. He fell to the side window. She saw his chest was still. She checked his pulse and felt nothing.

"Oh my gawd!" The old guy had the nerve to up and die on her in the middle of a lesson! What was she going to do? She didn't know how to land this thing!

Her insides clenched into a frozen mass of fear. All her muscles hardened, stiff as steel. With her chest clamped tight, it was hard to breathe.

She pushed the button on the yoke to talk on the radio, forcing her voice to work. "May day! May day! Someone help me. My instructor… I think he's dead."

A voice answered on the radio, "Aircraft calling May day, say call sign."

Jill looked at the little sign in front of her.

"N273G," she called on the radio.

"273 Golf ident," the voice on the radio said.

"Ident? I just did."

"Do you see an instrument in front of you that says the number

1200?"

"Yes," she said.

"Push the little button on it."

Jill did.

"273 Golf, ident observed on radar. You are three miles southwest of Edwards Air Force Base. Turn to a heading of 180."

Jill knew how to do that. She made the little airplane symbol on the instrument in front of her point toward the numbers 18. She looked at Old Vern and her chest stung. She had never been this close to a dead person before. Not even to Dad.

"I want… I need to land now," Jill said over the radio. She was starting to freak out. She couldn't catch her breath. Maybe the cockpit had run out of oxygen. Maybe Vern had died from lack of oxygen. She tried to take a deep breath as the thought of passing out scared the crap out of her.

"It's better if you can make it to an airport. You could get seriously hurt if you don't land at an airport. We can help you get down safely. The closest airport is the one five miles straight ahead of you. We'll have an ambulance waiting. What type of aircraft are you?"

"Diamond."

Jill's hands were slipping off the stick from sweat. Yet she was shivering.

"Do you see the airport in front of you?" The controller on the radio said.

"Yes."

"Have you ever landed before?"

"No," her voice cracked.

"We'll talk you through it."

Jill held her breath. How could some guy in a tower somewhere tell her how to land an airplane?

10 Squawking Emergency

Shaking with fright, Jill turned toward the airport ahead and to the left.

"What's your airspeed?" The voice over the radio sounded comfortingly calm. Jill was about to bring this bird down and the voice sounded like he was talking to just another pilot flying about, not a girl who didn't know a thing about how to land an airplane.

She looked at the only instrument that had "mph" on it. "100 miles per hour."

"Okay, you need to slow down. Pull back some on the throttle."

Jill pulled out the throttle. The propeller sputtered and the engine got quiet. Too much. She pushed it back in some. She watched the airspeed drop like crazy. Then she noticed she had the nose pointed up. The stall alarm went off. Jill pushed the nose down. A wave of nausea broke over her. She was scared to death and wishing she had never got in this plane. She wished she was safely on the ground holding her sisters. There wasn't anyone who could get her out of this but herself. No one could climb up in this airplane and take over. She had to do it all herself and it was pretty likely that what she did in the next few minutes would get herself killed. She gulped, forced a slow breath and tried to focus on flying. She remembered what Claire said about not freezing up. She had to pull it together and deal.

"Hold 80 miles per hour and lower two nicks of flaps to twenty degrees."

Huh? Jill saw the lever labeled flaps but she didn't know what the controller was talking about. She pushed it twice.

"273 Golf, you're a little high. Take a little more power off and keep your nose pointed down toward the runway."

Jill adjusted the throttle and stick.

"273 Golf, acknowledge."

"I'm scared."

"273 Golf, what's your name?"

Jill froze. She couldn't tell them her name. She didn't have permission to take lessons. And she can't let Mom find out. She was probably in big trouble too for flying into restricted airspace or whatever. Maybe it was her fault Old Vern kicked the bucket. Maybe her flying scared him into a heart attack. Whatever, she just knew she couldn't give them her real name.

She said the first thing that came to mind. "Angie Pitt."

"Angie, you're doing fine. You're almost there. Just keep lining up with that runway and keep descending, but don't let your airspeed get too fast. You should be at 70 miles per hour now."

Jill looked at the airspeed and it said 100 again!

"I'm going too fast."

"Angie, pull the throttle back, but keep your nose pointed down at the runway. You're getting close now."

Jill could see that. The runway was right in front of her. She saw firetrucks and an ambulance rush toward the runway.

"Angie, take all the power off now. Pull the throttle all the way off."

As Jill did, the airplane become quieter but it was still way too fast. She forced the nose down. She just wanted this nightmare to be over.

The plane impacted the ground and bounced back up. She shoved it down again and it ricocheted against the ground. In a wild ride, it bounced up and down again, getting worse, diving down and flinging up. She held on for dear life.

This time when the plane bounced back down, it hit the prop into the asphalt and broke the nose wheel off. The plane crashed to a stop. She lurched forward into her shoulder harness and inflating air bag.

Jill checked herself. Soaked in sweat, she was in one piece but her chest hurt. She looked at Old Vern. Poor Old Vern. But there was nothing she could do for him and she had to get out of there before the firetrucks and ambulance caught up.

She ripped off her harness and headset and bolted out the broken door. She ran fast, down a ditch and behind a building. She kept running without looking back. She thought she heard someone yelling behind her, but it could have been the sirens and the wind... and the blood rushing through her temples faster than a hurricane.

11 Identifier Lights

"Girl, I can't believe you," Nikka said a little too loudly.

"Shhh," Jill crunched down in the seat of Nikka's mom's Prius. "Just drive. I'll explain on the way home."

Nikka drove them out of the gas station where she had picked up Jill and onto the freeway ramp.

"Why am I picking you up in this lovely desert town? Are you running away again? Cuz you got farther in second grade when—"

"I took a flying lesson. I took someone's flying lesson when they didn't show up. But Old Vern was just standing there telling me to hurry up and get in. He thought I was his afternoon flight student."

"No, you didn't."

"He croaked! He died. While we were up in the air. We crashed."

"What?" Nikka took her eyes off the road and stared at Jill. "Are you okay?"

Jill pointed at the car in front of them on the freeway. "Don't get in an accident while I'm fleeing for my life. Kind of defeats the point."

"What are you talking about? What happened?"

"I thought he was taking a nap. He kept closing his eyes after he told me what to do. 'Climb to three thousand.' Snooze. Snooze. 'Descend to two.' Snooze. Snooze. Then I heard voices on the radio say we were in forbidden airspace and I had to land the plane by myself. I had to land — if you can call it that. The plane is wrecked. When the firetrucks came, I ran."

"Why?"

"Mom would kill me if she found out I was flying."

"You left an accident with a dead guy and you're worried about your mom."

"You know how my mom is."

Nikka was quiet for a moment. "What if they think there was something going on that was wrong. Like foul play or something. It looks suspicious that you left. It's like hit and run. You're supposed to stay and talk to the authorities."

"I couldn't. I didn't hit anyone. I don't know, I just bolted."

"Do they have any idea who was in the plane with him?"

"I told the guys on the radio a fake name: Angie Pitt."

"Very original. Wonder how long it will take them to figure that one out."

"Angelina Jolie is the only living famous woman pilot I know of. It just popped in my head."

"Yeah, she's a pilot. You're not even a student pilot. You could have died."

"Give me a break. I didn't know my instructor was going to die. I'm fine. My chest hurts a little from the seatbelt but that's all."

Nikka looked at her with wide eyes, like she had death on her. "I can't believe you. It's just your luck. How could you have so much crap happen to you? You've got a cloud of doom over your head or something. You should stay in your room more."

"Like my mother. No thank you. If my number is up, it's up. I'd rather die from adventure than bedsores and boredom."

"You should at least stay away from the airport for a while. They'll be pissed. They'll be looking for a girl terror in the skies. The Dead Daddy excuse only works for so long."

"Tell that to my mother." Jill sank in her seat. "It's not like I could have done anything for Vern. He was older than TV! He went out in his favorite place, the sky. He had a billion hours up there. Can you imagine? That's living. I think it was the way he wanted to go." Jill's tone changed.

Nikka looked at her worried. "Don't get any ideas. You have a lot to do, like go to college with me. You talked me into it. I don't even need college for art, but I'm going because you told me I had to be your roomie. You can't desert me now."

"Don't worry. There's been enough of the Grim Reaper around here. I'm just saying he had a good life."

"You're going to give up flying now, aren't you?"

"Why? Because it's totally dangerous and I suck at it, it costs a ton of money, which I don't have, and my mother forbids it?"

"No, cuz I can't be driving all around picking you up wherever you crash." She smiled reassuringly. "This thing isn't four-wheel drive, you know?"

12 Cleared For Immediate Takeoff

Rubbing her burning eyes, Jill took a break from studying flight radio procedures to gaze at her ceiling. She loved how her room with its medium blue walls made her feel like she was in the sky. Floating free from any entanglements. No sadness. No loneliness. No dead fathers. No broken mothers. No scared, fighting sisters. Simply the sky and its eternity.

She had heard the color of the soul was blue. That underneath we're all the same color.

"Life goes on," she told the mirror as she rubbed her eyes. She wouldn't let the heaviness set in. Not when she still had an hour free before her sisters got home. The neighbor Ms. Collins had taken them to Sunday school and pizza. One hour left before she was buried with responsibilities. She bolted for the door. On the way out, she grabbed Dad's treasured watch, his super expensive chronometer, from his special leather box inside his desk. She was prepared to do whatever it took to change her land-locked existence, even if it meant trading Dad's watch for flight lessons. He didn't need it anymore.

After the shock of crashing the Diamond had worn off, Jill was even more hooked on flying. If she had known how to land, maybe she could have gotten Old Vern help faster.

Biking around the airfield, Jill saw the windsock going crazy. One second it was pointing east and the next west. Could Claire fly in this wind?

Except for the occasional radio announcement by a passing plane, the lobby was quiet. The clerk, Marilee, was answering questions for a couple of pilots and handing them information aids about flying out of the one of the highest airports in California.

Jill quietly crept out the lobby doors and onto the airfield, armed with her arsenal of ideas to crack Claire today. Persistence hadn't worked, since she stopped by every day after school and Claire kept saying no to free lessons.

Clutching Dad's watch, she crossed the temporary tie-down area where people could park their planes while they used the facilities. The gas pumps were unoccupied so she kept going.

When she reached Claire's hangar, the wall-sized door was open wide. The sunlight illuminated a ton of greasy engine parts on stained workbenches. It was so full that Claire couldn't park her plane in there. Since she had the corner hangar, she was allowed to park it in front. The airport manager had installed a tie down spot toward the edge of the pavement for her.

Jill slithered inside and gazed at the poster on the back wall of a woman dressed in a snowsuit and flying goggles, leaning against a large, silver antique aircraft.

Claire noticed Jill and sighed. "You're an old dog who won't go home."

"The treats are better here." Jill searched the bottom of the poster for a title.

"That's Teresa James," Claire said. "1934. On her first solo cross-country, she got lost. Landed in a wheat field and asked the farmers for directions."

"I hope I do better than that."

"We have more navigational tools nowadays. GPS, landmarks, radar, aerial maps."

"Who? What?"

"You can read about it. Do I look like an encyclopedia?"

Man, was she in a mood today. In all the times since the Young Eagles flight that Jill had hung around Claire's hangar, this day needed a danger sign. Jill wondered if she should leave, but then felt Dad's watch dangling from her wrist and the hole in her heart. She took a deep breath.

"How do you know how to stay out of air that's restricted? It's kind of weird someone can own airspace."

With a torque wrench, Claire struggled against a bolt that wouldn't budge. "There's these great things called books that actually contain all the wisdom humans have been able to acquire so far. Fancy that."

Claire braced her feet against a sparkling silver engine and pulled at a bolt harder. Her face turned red and veins popped out of her forehead.

Today wasn't the best day to work on Claire. She wasn't exactly in the best frame of mind. Jill heard a plane take off on the runway and decided to try anyway. "What'ya doing?" Jill asked, peering over Claire's shoulder at the engine block.

Frustrated, Claire stopped pulling at the bolt and dropped the wrench. "We're not going to do this again," Claire said. "Didn't you say your mom won't let you fly? She may be right, you know. It isn't easy making a living as a pilot." She went back at the stuck bolt, huffing, and then said under her breath, "I should know."

"I am a pilot. Just no one knows it yet. You could help that."

Claire moved to her tool chest and searched through the wrenches. It didn't seem like she was paying attention to anything but wrenches.

Jill spoke up louder, "'Help me, Obi-Wan Kenobi. You're my only hope.'" She set the chronometer on the table next to the guts of an airplane. But as soon as it was off her wrist, she missed it. She didn't know if she could part with Dad's watch.

Claire didn't even look up. "You solve my problems, I'll solve yours. No one helped me. And I still have the debt to prove it. I guess we can't all be born with resources." Claire nodded her head in the direction of the hangar next door. Jill had noticed a green, yellow and red Grumman Tiger in there when the door was open. Claire laid into a bolt and grunted as she pulled at the wrench. "Some of us have to work for every little—" she grunted. Jill was glad she couldn't speak momentarily. Jeez, when that woman ranted, she really could rant.

Jill considered which tactic to try next as she circled a silver husk sitting on the floor, the beginnings of a cockpit. "Why're you building a plane?" She inspected the rivet holes.

An older man in a greasy jumpsuit walked in, waving a mallet. "She thinks she needs to expand her business. Stay small, I tell her, but who listens to their father?" He had kind eyes, a peppered beard and slightly round belly.

"I'm only trying to pay for my overhead." Claire gestured to the hangar, then pointed to an airplane seat sitting in the corner. "When one of these puppies costs five thousand dollars…" She shook her head.

"Wow. A five-thousand dollar seat?" Jill looked at it closely. Maybe it was made of something special. It wasn't.

"Watch out for this one, Jack" Claire motioned to Jill, "or she'll be bugging you to take her for a flight."

"That'd be kind of hard," Jack said, "since I'm not a pilot and I don't have a plane. It's good when your children surpass you." He smiled proudly.

Claire grunted and struggled with a part she couldn't free. "As if you ever did anything stupid enough to sabotage your whole career."

Jack's face clouded over with pain. He looked like a dam about to break, but he shook it off instead and sighed. He squatted next to the engine block and installed a magneto.

Wheeling on a stool, Claire rolled over to another toolbox and picked through it, sneaking glances at her father to suss out what he was thinking. Jack put his hand beneath the steel mass of the engine. Smash, it rolled down off the jack and onto the concrete floor.

"Owh! My hand!" Jack yelled. "Help me!" It looked like he was pinned. Claire ran to him and tried to lift the massive machinery. He slipped his hand out of a cavern, ripping with hearty laughter. "Got ya!" He waved his uninjured hand at her.

"You old fart." Claire rolled her eyes and returned to her toolbox.

"Now I know where you get it from," Jill said to Claire.

As if nothing had happened, Jack pulled a compass out of his pocket and set it on the table.

"Exactly how much did you have to hock to get the new parts?" Claire asked.

"Only my Ford," Jack said.

"You sold your car?"

"Eh, I didn't need that old thing anyway. Where do I ever go?"

"Just as long as you don't sell your house to buy the propeller, Dad."

"Eh, you do what you can..." Jack sanded a hole in a metal sheet. "It's only been my home for the last thirty years. That's all."

"You better not sell your house."

"That's what a good father I am — willing to sacrifice everything for my darling daughter. My one and only," Jack teased.

"I just don't want you moving in with me."

Jill enjoyed their banter. She remembered how good it felt to argue with Dad about little things. She felt herself weakening as she stood next to Jack, so she moved to the edge of the hangar and looked up. A jet roared by above them.

"That's a Seven Forty-Seven," Claire said.

"How high is it?" Jill asked.

"It's going west so I'd say about 34,000 feet."

"Wow. Do you fly that high?"

"No. I'd need oxygen on board above 14,500 feet."

"Or at 12,000 feet if you're sane," Jack said

"A little oxygen deprivation never hurt anyone," Claire said.

"She's kidding," Jack said. "Lack of oxygen can make you pass out."

"Only if you're a wimp," Claire said

"I'd do anything to fly. Did I mention that?" Jill put the chronometer back on her wrist. She twisted her arm, looking at all angles of the expensive, platinum timepiece. No one noticed. Jack was fitting an instrument into a hole in the metal sheet and Claire was trying to pluck a wire out of a small tube. Jill anticipated that she needed some needle-nose pliers and handed them to her.

"I could help out around here — be your gopher, your apprentice, your slave," Jill said dramatically. She hoped she didn't sound as pathetic as she felt She hoped she was only sounding amusing, but Claire didn't look amused. Her eyebrows were knit together as she concentrated on separating tiny wires. "I could help…"

"The only help I need is with my bank account." Nevertheless, she motioned for Jill to grab an end of the wing and move it out of the way. Jill was happy to assist.

"Don't you want to pass on all your superior-ness?" Jill asked. "I want to learn everything you know, oh Great Wise One of the Skies." Jill smiled sweetly. Who could resist an eager student? She couldn't bring herself to offer Dad's watch. It felt good around her wrist. Almost like she could still feel him, like she could still smell his cologne on it. She couldn't give it up.

She tried again, "You know you're the best pilot around. Not to mention the only flight instructor on the mountain now." Old Vern's passing had left the town without a qualified teacher, except Claire. As Jill thought of this, she felt more desperate. Claire really was her only hope. "It's your humanitarian duty."

Claire sighed. "Do you know what happens when you have a headwind?"

"It slows you down," Jill answered. She knew she got it right because Claire's eyebrow raised slightly.

"What happens when you have a strong headwind on takeoff or landing?" Claire asked.

Jill thought hard. She shrugged.

"Well," Claire said, "that would be something good for you to know if you're going to be a pilot."

Jill beamed. "You'll take me up? Teach me?"

"We'll talk about it when you have permission and the money to pay me." Claire hammered at a stuck fusion of two pieces of aluminum.

"That's messed up," Jill said. It just came out.

"That's life."

Claire slammed her finger with the hammer and screamed.

Jill left feeling her pain. She couldn't be mad at Claire for turning her down again. She understood Claire's sitch, which was sort of like hers. She had stuff to do and didn't have time for things that would keep her down.

13 Crosswind

"Oh, so, this you'll show up for?" Nikka asked. She was already deep into her aerobic regime by the time Jill met her in the school gym. That's where they ate lunch on Mondays. Nikka had a thing about having a working meal after the weekends.

To welcome Jill, Nikka spread a blanket out on the hard floor and scattered Tupperwares in a circle. Jill sniffed some sautéed tofu and stifled a cringe. She took a nibble, grateful she didn't have to make her own lunch, even if it was bean curd.

"This isn't good for your digestion." Jill sat on an exercise ball and did stomach crunches between bites.

"Why not?" Nikka chomped some asparagus and rolled the ball inward with her feet from a frog stance. "Birds eat on the run. So do New Yorkers."

"After you exercise yourself to death, I'll be sure you win the lifetime achievement award for tightest abs." Jill stopped the motion and watched Nikka.

"I'm certainly winning sainthood talking to you after you ditched me Saturday night." Nikka switched to another calisthenic with her side draped over the ball.

"I told you I was exhausted and fell asleep. No decent, self-respecting person could fall asleep before eight o'clock at night no matter what they're studying. I'm sorry. I'm sorry. I'm sorry. What can I say? I'll go in the Bestfriend Hall of Shame."

Nikka launched her foot above her head rhythmically. "I survived without you. The committee voted in favor of my green fuel rally next month. You still have a chance to make up some karma with me."

"Oh, good, because I was getting quite concerned about that."

"Your karma or green fuel?"

Jill was staring at a strawberry, not able to hear Nikka over all the loud thoughts hammering her head. Nikka knocked her off the exercise ball.

"Where are you?" Nikka asked.

"I really have a hard time doing physics homework when I'm going to be dead in a few decades anyway. What's the point?"

"Everyone has trouble doing physics homework. You need to get out. Have some fun."

"Fun? What's that? I think the word is even banned in my house."

Robbie swaggered into the gym and across the basketball court. He disappeared into the locker room, not seeming to observe the picnickers.

"I think he noticed you that time," Nikka said. "His head slightly moved in this direction — maybe that was just a tick."

"Shut up," Jill laughed. "If it's in the cards, he'll just start talking to me, right?"

Nikka threw herself around on the exercise ball, possessed by an evil spirit of extreme health and fitness. "Fate is the power you possess, to your own self, bless."

"Huh? Sometimes I don't even understand what you're saying."

"It's my level of profundity." Nikka's mouth curved up at the corners.

"You mean, curmudgeon-ity." Jill looked at the door Robbie had disappeared into and promised herself that the next time she saw him, she would do whatever it took to get his attention. What did she have to lose?

"One of the things I love about you is your non-1984 vocab, but I'm pretty sure curmudgeon-ity isn't a word. Try again, Genius."

"Killjoy."

Nikka switched to a deep bend. "Oh, I forgot to tell you. I found something in my room that your dad gave you."

"What?" Jill asked.

"You're not ready. I put it in your room. You'll find it when you're ready."

"What is it?"

"You're not ready."

"What I'm not ready for is fifth period. I haven't finished my homework." Jill gathered the Tupperwares and put them in Nikka's bag. "See you in class."

"You can quote me. In your paper."

"Too profound," Jill teased. "I don't want to scare anyone."

* * *

At the ski resort, Jill crunched across the snow sporting her new Volcum beanie. She didn't know if she could go through with it. She had a good plan but her pulse was roaring in anticipation. It made her feel a little sick. As she made her way up the sideline of the slope, she saw Nikka's booth for recycling awareness.

"The call of the cause got to you," Nikka said as she set out brochures and moved to the sound of her satellite speakers. With Jill's eyes latched on the run where snowboarders were competing, it was obvious Robbie was the center of her attention.

"Gotta do my part." Jill's eyes never left the slope as she sat on the table. Robbie was doing well in the Rail Jam, hitting the rails just right and sliding off into complete turns with solid landings. Even whizzing down the slope at death-defying speed, he could stop easily in a second before the line of spectators, in full control.

An unsuspecting junior high kid approached the booth. "Hey," he said to Nikka and raised his eyebrows up and down at her. He licked his lips. "Hey, Baby. You're hot."

Nikka thrust a picture of a landfill at him. "We're pigs who poop in our own pens. We only recycle thirty percent of our trash." Nikka held up a full garbage bag to demonstrate. "Each person makes five pounds of trash per day. Try to imagine the size of our landfills!"

Jill laughed hysterically at the expression on the kid's face as he walked away, confused, with a brochure on waste abatement in his hand.

She turned back to the slopes and spotted Robbie setting up for another trick, gliding toward a jib. He had a live-in-the-moment ease about him that melted the frost off her face and restored her ability to smile. She liked the way he looked — confident and in control. She had felt that once, too, when she was in the plane with Claire. Powerful.

After boardsliding a down-rail jib, Robbie spun a 360 in the quarterpipe, stomped a solid landing and skidded to a stop in front of the judges. His friends banged his helmet in appreciation. His buddy Trevor pounded his fists. As Robbie freed himself from his helmet and popped his feet out of his bindings, the judges announced him as the winner. Jill sauntered over closer to him and listened to him encourage the guy who came in last.

"I washed out on the last landing," the guy complained, looking at the ground and hunching over, trying to hide within his own shoulders.

"Yeah, but you had some style on the tricks you did land." Shrugging, like it was no biggie, Robbie banged sticky snow off his board. "Everybody washes out sometimes. No one's dialed in on every trick."

The guy emerged from his hunched shoulders like a turtle coming out of his shell. He looked up and nodded.

Jill moved closer to Robbie and was about to open her mouth when a mass of snowboarders chanted "Pizza, Pizza," and surrounded them like savages circling a deer on a spit.

Jill said, "Hey," to Robbie, but the pizza chant drowned her out.

"Not pizza again," Robbie said. "Barbecue. Let's go to Brad's BBQ." Robbie left, brushing fast past Jill. No debate, all the guys followed him without question, even though thirty-degree weather doesn't make for the best picnic by the lake. They took off in their cars racing out of the parking lot like insano's on a goofy TV race for a million bucks.

Jill returned to Nikka's booth, disappointed she didn't get to talk to Robbie. She had two funny things prepared to say and everything.

"What happened to Robbie this year?" Nikka asked. "Last year he wasn't even on the field. This year he's the leader of the lemmings."

"It's not hard to figure out how to be popular. It's all in attitude and hygiene," Jill laughed. "If you want to be popular, of course. Aren't famous people always the ones who didn't fit in at high school?"

"Whatever." Nikka turned up her radio and bopped around the booth. Jill sat on a carton and watched the magic. Nikka was made of vibrating waves of rhythm. No stiffness or inhibitions destroyed her pulse. Like seaweed undulating, Nikka graced her body into the flow of the music. It was fun to watch her dissolve into melody. She wished she could move like that.

After the song was over, Jill stood up. "Sorry I can't stay any longer," Jill said. "I have to go take care of the snotty-nosed brats and Zombie Mommy."

"I know. Thanks for coming. The Pleiadians totally took notice and added you to the mothership roster. Now you're guaranteed a spot on the escape pods before the world explodes."

"Whew." Jill wiped imaginary sweat off her brow. "I'll sleep good tonight." She hugged Nikka.

"Look in your room," Nikka said.

"What are you talking about?"

"Remember, I told you I found something your dad had given you and put it back in your room so you'd find it when you're ready?"

"Oh yeah. So you've decided I'm ready?"

Nikka nodded.

"What is it?"

"You'll see."

14 Maximum Glide

Evenings brought Jill even more chores. When Mrs. Collins dropped off the girls from after-school daycare, Jill made sure they ate and had baths. She marveled at how she could fool the world that everything was all right with her family simply by washing. Clean clothes, clean noses, clean dishes. No one bothered them, or threatened to disband their family. A dysfunctional mother had to be better than a foster mother, a stranger.

Jill tackled a colossal pile of laundry as she microwaved dinner and read from a flying book — talk about multitasking. The screaming match between her sisters provided lovely background noise. She balanced folded laundry and a plate of chow, and banged into Mom's bedroom.

Mom was still lying in bed, of course. She hadn't moved much.

"Mom?" Jill plopped down the food. "Please eat something."

Mom raised up a little on her pillows. Her night shirt was stained again already.

Jill wanted to give Mom a Dr. Phil-style kick-in-the-butt and tell her to snap out of it. But she sat next to her instead.

"How you feeling?" Jill asked.

"Thanks for doing the laundry and cooking. You'll make a good housewife someday."

"I'm a housewife now. Remember how you wanted this job? You love the domestic goddess thing. I have other dreams. This one's yours. Remember?"

"There's a house, but no wife anymore." Mom rolled away from her.

Jill knew she had to change the subject before Mom started crying. Maybe Jill's passion could distract her. "Did you know you don't have to have a college degree to fly commercial? It'll be a bummer to miss all those keggers but I would gladly give up my wild and crazy college days to use my college fund for flight school."

"Hmm?" She turned away more.

Jill reclined next to her and put her feet up on the laundry pile. "Well, if you're going to insist, I could go to a college with an aviation program. But I really think I'm one of those one-track trains, don't you? Getting all my ratings will be expensive enough. There's the multi-engine rating, the instruments rating, the ..."

Mom rolled over and looked at her. "How could you?" Her face was tattooed with old reddened tear streaks. "You want to take risks after what I've been through? Are you trying to follow your father?"

"Oh, please." Jill sat up. "Dad never got to fly, either. He didn't take risks. He had an accident, Mom. It was an accident. Accidents happen."

"I don't understand you, Jill. Why do you want to fly? What are you trying to prove? Or are you trying to hurt me more?"

"Like I could." When Jill saw the shocked expression on Mom's face, she knew she had crossed a line. She ran out of the room.

Jill paced the living room, kicking toys. She punted the Pinocchio DVD clear into the kitchen. Yeah, right. Wish upon a star and your dreams come true. Not when you're Mom's prisoner.

Her sisters announced their presence to the living room with yelps. Jill ran outside on the patio to breathe. To see the sky. Why did she have to want to fly so much? Her dream was too big — unattainable. Who did she think she was? She was crazy to think she could handle an airplane all by herself. She couldn't even drive a car yet. Mom still refused to let her take Driver's Ed. She probably never would.

Jill paced around the pine trees and kicked pinecones. There's no way through a five-foot-thick reinforced-steel wall. Banging her head against Mom was only giving her a headache. She was sick of it. Mom had always been the barrier that boxed her in, safely tucked under a pound of plumage so Mother Hen could feel in control. And now it was unbearable.

She booted a pinecone against a tree, and it cracked apart, sending spiky shrapnel everywhere. The scent of sap stopped her. She picked up another prickly cone and sniffed. It reminded her of something.

She recalled her favorite ritual. Saturday mornings with Dad, their special time, set aside from the best part of the week. It didn't matter where they went. They just got out and enjoyed —a day where work was banned and Dad didn't feel guilty about not working. She remembered the roads that wound around the mountain ridges, with sunlight peeking through the pine trees. Driving with open windows, they breathed in the refreshing fragrance of damp earth and fallen needles. Fresh-scented forest filled with sappy pinecones.

She drop-kicked the pinecone and leaned against a trunk. She couldn't believe she was powerless to ever talk to Dad again. The permanence of that barrier was something she knew for sure would never change. All she could do was remember him.

A dragonfly landed on her toe. She looked closely at its black eyes and horizontal double wings. As it slowly waved its appendages, she contemplated the two sets of wings and what a good design they were for smooth flight — placed perfectly on its long body for just the right balance. Its tail was the perfect rudder for stability.

She was wondering how long it was going to sit there when her sisters came running out of the house and onto their yard vehicles, noisy plastic-wheeled abominations. As the ruckus scared away the dragonfly, she watched it fly gracefully, magically, to a pine tree and disappear amongst the pinecones. The little insect made flight look so easy.

Dragonflies spend most of their lives in larval form. The story of her life.

Jill shook it off and joined her sisters. Big Wheels. That's the ticket. No one could stop her from driving a Big Wheel. Bre and Kelly laughed as Jill tried to cram her body into the tiny tricycle and pedal without hitting her butterflied knees on the handle bars.

15 Attitude Indicator

In the morning as Jill dressed in black for school, she noticed her jewelry box was open. She looked inside it to see if her sisters had taken anything. She didn't find anything missing but she did discover something she hadn't seen since her own caveman days, when she communicated with shrill sounds and blunt objects, like the cute young barbarians across the hall. Back in the day, she collected small pieces of jewelry for a charm bracelet. Dad gave her a dragonfly charm and she forgot about it until now. This must be what Nikka had found and returned to her room for when she was "ready."

She picked up the silver- and blue-winged trinket and remembered how special she had felt when Dad bought it and attached it to her bracelet. He liked to switch around what nickname he'd call her, and for a while after he bought the charm, he called her 'GonFly. She put it in her pocket, hoping it would bring her good luck — an airplane ride, a date with Robbie, world peace.

But her only mission for the moment was to make it to school before the bell rang, announcing another day of entrapment.

In biology class, Jill spaced out. She'd never need this stuff being a pilot. She fingered the dragonfly charm in her pocket. She remembered now. The dragonfly charm entered her life on a Saturday morning.

A couple of years ago, the whole family was camping in the oak patch that sprawled halfway down the mountain. Her sisters and mother had gone to bed in the tents and Jill sat around the campfire with Dad. He looked sad. He ran his fingers through his thick, cropped hair absentmindedly as he hunched down on a log. His black-frame glasses hung down midway on his nose, but he didn't bother hitching them back up.

"What ya thinking?" Jill asked.

"To be honest," Dad said, "I'm thinking I don't like my job."

"Why?" Jill skewered a marshmallow with a stick.

"I'm just not into it. I can't really explain it. It just makes me feel empty. I always wonder what it would have been like if I had gone after what I really wanted to do."

"What was that?" She roasted the marshmallow to a perfect browning.

"What does it matter now?" He threw a stick in the fire. "It's too late for me to start at zero and work my way up in a different profession, Jill. What's done is done."

That was the first time Jill realized Dad had been looking melancholy after work. She had seen him wear that joyless face before but hadn't really thought much about it. Some of his routines had changed too. He had stopped going to the gym but he still looked fit. It was just that he didn't stand quite as tall anymore.

"Some people don't know what they want to do, so they do whatever falls into their lap," he said. "I think it would be better to try on different things and find out in the doing of them. If you start gathering that information when you're young, you can make a better decision when you are pushed out of the nest. You'll have an idea of what you want to explore. You don't have to decide now, Jill, but do collect your preferences. Figure out what you like and don't like. Because being stuck in something you don't like…"

Jill was ready for this conversation to be over. She didn't know how to make Dad feel better. It did seem like it was too late for him. That made her incredibly sad.

The next morning he bought her the dragonfly charm in town when they had cheated during their camping trip by going to the store twenty miles away for prepackaged food. So much for roughing it.

Her biology teacher brought her mind back to class, announcing a test. Jill pulled out a piece of paper from her notebook and drew a line down the center. On the left side she wrote, "Likes" and on the right "Dislikes." Under Likes, she wrote: flying, dragonflies, Robbie, blue. And under Dislikes, she wrote: walls.

16 Turn and Slip

It was too much. Bre and Kelly were howling and jumping on Mom's bed. Jill grabbed a bottle of pills from Mom's night table and slammed them in the trash. The doctor prescribed them faster than she could trash them. Was he getting a commission from the drug companies? Jeez, he was worse than the friendly neighborhood drug dealer. Too bad the doctors didn't try this stuff out on themselves first. To be fair, they didn't know what was going on at home. Jill wasn't exactly broadcasting it because a sedated parental pod had to be better than breaking up her family in foster care. What if she never got to see her sisters again?

After Jill got her sisters to sleep, complete with plenty of stories and kisses, she closed the door to her bedroom and took out a sheet of paper, the legal release for flying lessons. Under "parent or guardian," Jill signed Mom's name. She folded it up and put it away in her backpack. She'd have to take matters into her own hands, direct her own destiny. She was tired of being fate's prey, a victim of circumstance. As much as she loved her mother, the woman had gone completely mad and it didn't seem like she had any intention of coming back from Never-Neverland. This was the right decision. It was time to take control. Hey, it couldn't get any worse, could it?

* * *

Nikka had a new Pilates move and was flopping around in the living room. Jill put some ankle weights on and moved her legs around half-heartedly. The tunes were low to avoid waking her sisters.

"I don't know how I let you talk me into things," Jill said. "No one else gets away with that. You're up to your old Jedi mind tricks."

"That's why we've been friends for so long," Nikka said between flops. "We know how to manipulate each other."

"I don't manipulate you."

"What about Coastal Cleanup Day? I totally missed doing my part," Nikka said it with a self-mocking smile, "because you guilted me into babysitting. They are cute, though."

"Want 'em? We're having a special this year. You can have them both for two dolla'."

"No, thanks. I have much sowing of the wild oats to do before staying home with the kids."

"Yeah, where were you last night? I snuck out of lockdown and went by your house, but you weren't there," Jill accused.

"Caesar spontaneously took me down the hill to a dance contest. He's got the hot moves. I wish he could talk to me the way his body does. Yesterday, he said I had a nice nose. Romantic, huh? I was all like swooning in my Skechers." Nikka looked like a large fish trying to get back in water. "I don't even know if he likes me. I'm probably just another dance partner to him, teaching me new moves like you teach a dog to shake." She demonstrated.

"What do you call that move?"

Nikka paused a moment and tapped her belly. "Off the hook. These abs are steel."

"It's important to have body parts similar to auto parts. So huggable. Did you win? The contest?"

"Second place. First prize was a gift certificate for Whole Foods."

"All the couscous and quinoa you can eat. I can't believe you didn't win."

"It takes a while to break in a new partner." Nikka stretched in a back bend like a trained seal. "What are you wearing?" She pointed to Jill's wrist.

"That's what I wanted to show you. It's my dad's chronometer." Jill belly-flopped to the floor and did backward leg lifts.

"What's a chronometer?"

"It keeps time precisely. With great accuracy. Exactly, to be precise. It reminded him of the relativity of time."

"A watch that keeps exact time?"

"It was a joke to him. Ironic. Daylight Savings proves time is relative. He said wearing this watch reminded him that time is actually not an absolute and that there is no time in eternity."

"Then why'd he work so hard all the time? He was never

around. I hardly knew him," Nikka joked. It was a sketch she performed with him when he was alive. Nikka would complain that she never got to see him and he would respond that he was planning on retiring early, enjoying life after he made his fortune, and making it up to her. He hugged her when he came home from work, just like his other girls.

Nikka didn't have a father around and Jill hadn't minded sharing hers. She liked having someone along when they went out to eat on family night. It evened up the table: her sisters fought over crayons and dolls, her parents fought over bills and shopping lists, and she and Nikka fought over vegetables and animal flesh. Jill had taken it for granted that since Nikka fit into the family, she would always be a part of it. Now there weren't any family dinners for her either.

"He inherited it." Jill took the chronometer off her arm and placed it gently on the table. "Do you know how much one of these suckers cost? Ten thousand. He always wondered if he should sell it, even though it was his—" Jill felt a presence in the room and looked up toward the hallway.

Bre stood there in wet pajamas. Jill went to her and carried her back to her room. "It's my night off. No crises tonight. Remember?"

Bre was strangely silent. Usually she whined when she had an accident. Tonight she stayed still and rigid in Jill's arms. Her eyes were distant.

"Bre, Little Bean, what's wrong? What's a matter?" Jill set her down in her room and stripped the pink ruffly PJs off her, retrieving the pizza-stained rainbow jammies from the dirty clothes pile. Bre was hard to dress, so stiff and out of it. "Did something happen, Little Bean? Tell me. Was it a bad dream?"

Bre's eyes were open but unfocused. She looked like someone had pushed a button and turned her off. It was scaring Jill.

"You just had a bad dream. Go back to sleep." She put Bre back in bed, laying her on a towel and covering her up with dry blankets. She kissed her. "Close your eyes. Here's Mr. Bubba Bear." Bre rejected the teddy bear with a quick smack. The bear flew off the bed.

"Okay. Here's Doodles the Happy Dodo Bird." She handed her another stuffed animal, doing a happy Dodo dance. "See, Doodles is happy. Because he's a Dodo." Bre accepted the large bird as a bed mate. Jill kissed her forehead and both cheeks. She wanted to wrap her up in her arms and squeeze the sad out of her.

She turned off the light and slipped out.

Instead of returning to the living room, Jill went to her room and crawled in bed. After a few minutes, she felt Nikka scoot in next to her.

"I feel like everyone needs taking care of," Jill said. "What about me? No one takes care of me and I'm fine."

"You're strong. You have to be."

"Exactly. It's not fair."

"So what do you want? You want to fall apart too?"

"What's the point?" Jill rolled away and dropped off into the safe world of sleep, where nothing hurt, no one needed her and time didn't exist.

At breakfast as Jill made pancakes, she watched Bre. She was as normal as ever, giving her Do-do bird sips of her milk, which spilled down the front of the stuffed animal. It was almost a relief to hear her fight with Kelly over the orange juice.

Nikka cut up mountains of cantaloupe and strawberries. She had a slower sway to the music in the morning. "White flour isn't good for them. It sticks to their intestines."

"Good." Jill flipped a cake. "Maybe then they won't be hungry all day."

"White flour causes cancer."

"My dad ate right and he's dead." Jill flipped a pancake onto Kelly's plate and doused it with syrup.

Nikka didn't have anything to say to that.

Jill poured the last of the batter into one uber pancake that took up the entire pan and nearly threw the bowl in the sink, rushing to finish. "I gotta get a boatload of studying done today. I gotta know what I'm doing if I'm gonna take flying lessons soon." Under her breath, she added, "As soon as I get a bunch of money."

"Don't you have enough going on? You haven't had breakfast yet." Nikka fed Bre a piece of cantaloupe. Bre made an adorable face as her thank-you. Nikka squeezed her.

"You feed the children and make sure they eat the right things to live to a hundred and twenty. I'm gonna go set an airspeed record or something." Jill flipped the giant pancake and splattered some batter against the backsplash. "I don't need food. I need a pilot's license."

Nikka threw a hot pad at her.

"Thanks for babysitting," Jill said.

"Anytime. They're my sisters, too. I just wish you could hang with us. You're always going Mach 5."

"I'm sorry. I didn't pick this dream. It picked me." Jill scooped up her books from the table and headed out.

17 Isolated Thunderstorms

With her head under the cowling, Claire didn't notice Jill approaching her plane at the gas pumps.

"I learned about big headwinds in takeoffs and landings," Jill said, stalking her from behind the pump.

Claire knocked her head on the cowling and grimaced. She looked at Jill with her all-business stone-face as always. "What about it?" Claire checked an opening next to the propeller of her plane. She pulled out a bird's nest. "Not the smartest bird." She handed the nest to Jill.

"Cozy spot," she called back to Claire as she marched over to the bushes and set the nest down. "In a strong headwind, it takes less runway to take off. Very handy if the runway is short."

"Yes, and?"

"Same thing with landing. It helps you land and stop in a shorter distance. The wind is like a big hand pushing you along or stopping you in your tracks."

Claire checked the oil dipstick. "What do you need to know about altimeters?"

"They're often wrong so you have to adjust them all the time or you could fly into a mountain if you don't know how low you really are. You can set them to pressure, density or true altitude. I think it's so weird that they teach science is an absolute but there're all these inconsistencies. Relativities. How could there be more than one altitude? You're either high or you're not."

Claire laughed.

Jill smiled. That was the first time she had gotten a laugh out of Claire, and she wasn't even trying this time.

Claire regarded the spackling of clouds in the sky. It was March and still the snow hadn't arrived. It was plenty cold, but moisture avoided them. It made for good flying weather, though.

"You've been studying," Claire said. "Very good. You'll be a pilot in no time."

"Finally, a convert," Jill said. "I'm ready for flying lessons."

"You have the money and the signed permission form?" Claire heaved a ladder to her plane.

"Yep." She waved the forged paper. This had to work.

"I don't know about teaching, Jill. I need to catch up on my bills before they shut me down. Insurance since 9/11 is impossible. I don't know how anyone can afford to stay in business. Teaching is dangerous. Students will find a hundred ways to kill you." Claire climbed up the ladder with the gas hose and stuck the nozzle in the tank. "As soon as Jack and I have finished building my new plane, I can expand my business. Pick up more work... I hope."

"That's my hero. Able to leap tall obstacles in a single bound. I knew there was a reason I look up to you. That and you're standing on a ladder above me."

Regardless of Jill's demeanor, Claire was taking her seriously. "Don't look up to me. I'm no hero. I was so reckless, once, I paid dearly, and I'll keep paying for the rest of my life. Why do you think I'm working here?" Claire turned further away, scrutinizing the inside of the gas tank.

Jill dropped her smile. "Yeah, what happened? I heard you used to be an airline pilot."

"Never mind." Claire climbed down the ladder and put away the gas hose.

Jill sensed she should ease off. Whatever Claire's mistake was, it had obviously changed her life. Big Bear City wasn't exactly an aviation hub and she was sure instructing or charters or whatever she did couldn't pay anywhere near what airline flying pays. "When will your other plane be done?" Jill asked.

"Should be summer."

"Are you going to hire other pilots?"

"Maybe," Claire said.

Jill gave her the Eager Student Look.

Claire shook her head. "I can't trust just anyone. Especially around here." She said it with such finality that Jill didn't question it, even though she wanted to know what was wrong with the local pilots.

Claire stuck a clear vile into a spigot on the wing and checked the drips of gas for impurities. When she was done, Jill handed her the permission slip. "Time for a lesson?" She gave her a check from her own account that she prayed would be good. She had no idea what was in the account but she was hoping for the best.

Claire looked at the check and changed her mind. "Hop in." She opened the left-side door.

"You want me to sit in the pilot's seat?" Jill asked.

"If you're going to learn to fly this thing," Claire said, "you're going to have to sit in the pilot's seat. Just remember you are Pilot in Command when you sit in that seat. That means you make the decisions. It's your show. You accept full responsibility when you are Pilot in Command."

"Got it." Jill balanced on the step on the wheel and climbed in the seat. She fumbled with the seatbelt. Suddenly, she was nervous. The last time she was in a plane, it didn't end so well. The terror of the plane bouncing up and down on the runway was sending shivers down her spine. She willed her hands to steady and latch the seatbelt.

She knew how to attach the pieces together, she just couldn't get her hands to stop shaking and insert the loops. She tried to hide her clumsiness and hurry as Claire was plugging in her headset and adjusting it over her ears.

Jill bit at her bottom lip to calm down. She finally got her seatbelt latched. She was excited to sit in the pilot's seat, but it was also scary. What if she did something wrong that Claire couldn't fix?

"Turn on the master switch and pump the throttle three times," Claire said.

Jill did. Claire opened the window and yelled something that sounded like, "Claire!" Why were you supposed to yell your name before starting the propeller? Maybe so people would know who to blame if the six-foot spinning blade chopped up someone standing in front of the prop.

"Turn on the mags and push the start button."

As Jill did as instructed, the plane burst to life. "This little thing sure can make a lot of noise." She put on the headset Claire handed her.

Through the headset, Jill heard Claire say, "Take your feet off the brakes and let it roll forward."

Jill hadn't even realized her feet were smashing down the brakes all the way to the floor. She eased up and the plane rolled forward to the run-up area next to the beginning of the runway.

Jill looked at the runway next to them and felt her stomach sink.

It was too soon to take off. Shouldn't they spend another hour or two or three sitting here looking at it? Her heart was beating fast and her breathing couldn't keep up. She felt a little dizzy. It was something being in the pilot seat. She could feel the authority of the position. Maybe she wasn't ready for it.

Claire showed her how to run through the Before Takeoff checklist and then helped her line up the airplane at the end of the runway.

"Just put the throttle all the way in and keep the airplane lined up with the centerline at all times."

Jill slowly put the throttle in and the plane started ripping down the runway. They veered to the left and she quickly footed the rudder pedal on the right. Just as they were headed to roll off the right edge of the runway, Claire motioned for her to pull back on the yoke, the control column. Jill yanked it back and the plane shot up in the air.

Claire quickly pushed the yoke in. "Too much. You don't want to stall this close to the ground. Never pitch your nose up that high."

Jill felt where the yoke was and held it steady as she watched the pavement drop away beneath them. She looked behind at the shrinking airstrip and saw Jack waving from the flightline. He looked so small but his enthusiastic waves were huge gestures, with long shadows sweeping across the ground.

In a flash, they were over the lake, already completely away from the airfield. Where was the sonic boom? Jill felt there should be some kind of big blast celebrating the defeat of gravity. Lifting off the ground and becoming airborne was easy. Then why was she holding her breath? The best way she could explain it to herself was that it was easy and it was hard.

Anyway, the real trick was landing. Somehow she'd have to get this kite to slow down and stop flying onto a little patch of pavement. They gained altitude as they flew over the lake, still climbing after reaching one thousand feet above ground.

"Turn north," Claire said.

Jill found 360 degrees on the heading indicator and turned toward it. She watched the dial rotate as she turned.

"You have to roll out before you get to 360 or you'll go past it. When you're at about 350, level the wings."

Jill followed her instructions and got the plane to head north toward the mountain ridge. As they flew over it, Jill gazed down at the pine trees and saw the secret dirt roads she had never been on before.

Jill looked at the airspeed indicator and saw they were going 120 miles per hour. Twice the speed of a car. In less than five minutes, they were over the desert. The terrain dropped down and even though they were in straight and level flight, they were now four thousand feet above the ground instead of one. It was so cool. The land seemed to stretch out forever. Miles and miles of roads disappearing in the distance. Little clumps of housing areas and dry rivers were etched in the earth.

"Descend to two thousand."

Jill pushed the yoke forward and the nose pitched down. In less than two minutes they were close enough to see all the junk people ditched in the desert. Mattresses and couches leaned against cactus.

"Who leaves all this crap out here?" Jill asked.

"Everyone, looks like. I figure it biodegrades out here better than in a landfill. Nothing decomposes in a landfill."

"I know, I know," Jill said. "My friend Nikka is a big environmentalist. She says every diaper ever used is still sitting in a landfill somewhere. Isn't that gross?"

"Hey, go a little lower. I might could use that couch."

Jill took the plane closer to the couch Claire pointed at and then caught movement in her peripheral vision.

It was Claire cracking up. "Did you think we would land out here between the cacti and strap the couch on the top?"

"Since just half an inch of ice destroys fifty percent of the wings' lift, I'd say that would be a very bad idea. It's called aerodynamics. Even small things on the plane's surface ruin the aerodynamics."

Claire gave her a thumbs-up. Jill had found the one way to impress Claire Cabello: knowledge. "Climb to three thousand."

Jill raised the nose and found she had to give it more gas to keep from slowing down too much.

"The reason you wouldn't want to land out here is you'd have a very slim chance of surviving. On a hot day, Billy Bryson forgot about density altitude and smashed into terrain like this. He hit a rock and his face went through the panel. Nasty gash."

"He lived?"

"Some crashes are fatal. Some aren't."

Jill looked down at the terrain. There sure were a lot of plants that grew in sand, spotting the landscape for as far as she could see. The cactus and boulders looked like hard targets amidst the chaparral. She made a mental note to read up on density altitude.

"Are you ready to try a controlled stall?" Claire asked.

"Easy."

"Keep your hands on the yoke as I demonstrate." Claire pulled back on the yoke until the nose was extremely high.

Jill gasped. She could see nothing but sky out the window. She pushed the yoke in.

Claire pulled back some more. The plane slowed down and the wind stopped rushing around it. It was so much quieter, Jill could hear her heart pounding. She pushed against the yoke.

"Let it go up," Claire said.

But Jill kept pushing it back down. She couldn't help herself. She bit her lip.

"Let it go." They kept battling the yoke until Jill said, "But you said never to push the nose up that high."

"I'm trying to demonstrate to you what happens when you do. It's okay. Let the nose go up."

Jill let go and the plane pitched up. The stall alarm shrieked. Jill remembered that terrifying first flight moment, the first time she had ever heard a stall alarm go off. The nose of the plane dropped off to the left. It was like the worst drop-off on Space Mountain at Disneyland.

Jill suddenly lost it, hyperventilating. The alarm brought it all back. The terror, the helplessness. She felt claustrophobic strapped in tight, with no way out.

18 Situational Awareness

"**H**ard right rudder," Claire said.

The stall alarm was still screaming. With the nose wobbling, the plane didn't feel like it was flying anymore. Were they dropping out of the sky? Not if she could help it. Jill brought herself back and stomped the right rudder. Forcefully, she pushed down the nose.

"Not too much. Don't dive for it."

Jill released some pressure and they leveled out. She realized she was chewing her lip and stopped.

"See?" Claire asked. "Piece of cake. Nothing to it."

When Jill took her feet off the rudder, she noticed they were shaking. But it was true that this stall wasn't nearly as scary as her first real one. It kind of helps to know what to do about them in advance. And of course, having a flight instructor next to her made a difference. She tried to calm her shakes.

"Turn to the left, zero two zero degrees," Claire said. "When you turn, use a little rudder on the same side. It's called a coordinated turn."

Jill put her foot back on the rudder and turned the yoke while applying light rudder pressure. Her foot was still shaking so bad, she could hardly get it to stay on the pedal. She hoped Claire didn't see it.

"You doing okay?" Claire asked.

"Yep." Jill rolled out on the heading. "Piece of cake."

"That's enough for today. Head back and I'll show you how to grease a landing."

"You'll take over?"

"Yes. It takes a while to learn how to slow down the plane and get it to glide into a semi-stalled state. You have to nail it just right, especially airspeed. And gusty winds can push you off the runway if you're not careful. But you'll get it with practice. The more you do it, the more you'll have a feel for how it's supposed to be done. It takes time to understand the visual clues."

Claire corrected the mixture setting. "Once you have landings down as well as emergency procedures, stalls and a few other things, you'll be able to solo."

"As in, all by myself? Are there training wheels?" Now she was really freaked out — excited that one day she'd be able to handle a plane by herself but freaked out just the same.

"I won't let you solo until I know you're ready. Don't worry."

"When do most people solo? After how many flight lessons?"

"Depends. About ten to fifteen hours."

Whoa, how in the world would she be ready to fly an airplane alone after only fifteen hours of instruction? There was so much to learn.

"What makes an airplane bounce when it lands?" Jill asked.

"That's called porpoising. It's like a porpoise diving up and down."

"Yeah." Jill shuddered as she remembered her nightmare landing.

"It's from too much airspeed, especially in a low-wing airplane. Angle, too."

Jill wanted to ask more but didn't want to give herself away. Who knew what Claire would think if she found out Jill was the one who crashed the plane with Old Vern.

Following Claire's instructions, Jill made the airplane climb to pass above the mountains at a safe altitude. Right after the ridge, they could see the airport.

"Look carefully for traffic," Claire said. "Airport patterns are the busiest part of the sky."

"It's clear," Jill said. Reluctantly, she let Claire take control. She hated letting go.

"We've entered the Downwind Leg in the landing pattern," Claire said. "It's sort of an invisible lane in the sky, parallel to the runway but in the opposite direction of landing. Ninety-degree turn into Base and then again to Final Approach. A rectangle in the sky. Got it?"

Jill nodded enthusiastically. "I've studied that. I love the logic and order of flying."

Landing put Jill on the edge of her seat. She knew it was the hardest part. She had certainly seen how difficult it was to get right. She cringed when she remembered bouncing hard off the pavement.

As Claire lined up, soaring toward the centerline of the runway, Jill glanced at her high school below. She was pretty sure she could see

Robbie on the soccerfield. He was even cute when he was the size of a kumquat. And then she quickly put her attention back to the landing.

With the runway a few feet under the plane, Jill's heart pounded against her ribs like it was trying to get out. Claire closed in on the ground slowly. Jill gently rested her hands on the control column to feel Claire's dexterity — the pulling, pushing and turning that tamed the wings. She memorized it and was sure she could mimic it.

"I like to slow down as much as possible so she sinks softly into the ground," Claire said. She checked her instruments again and powered off. With a slight bump, she landed the plane and rolled the nose down. "Ta-da."

Jill heard it in her voice. It was still a thrill to her, even after thousands of landings.

Under her feet, Jill felt the brakes press down and the plane slowed almost to a stop. Claire taxied them over to her hangar and shut down in front of it, where she usually parked.

"You did good," Claire said.

"Thanks."

She'd made it through the lesson. Landing was as much of a mystery as ever, but it was totally fun that she was the one doing everything. Well, almost. Okay, not really.

Jill stepped out of the plane and groaned. All her muscles were tight and tense. Her legs felt wobbly and almost gave out when she tried to stand, but her head was still ten thousand feet up.

Claire was already at her hangar door. "Come by tomorrow after three and we'll get your paperwork done, get your student license." She disappeared inside.

Jill tried to walk but she still felt weak-kneed and wobbly. She noticed then that she was completely soaked in sweat. How nice. Good thing Robbie wasn't around.

Inside the airport lobby, Marilee was monitoring the radio as she filed paperwork. Marilee had teased red hair like a halo around her head. She wore a big green plastic bead necklace and a gray sweatshirt layered with lace that hung off her shoulder.

"How'd you do?" Marilee asked. Closer up, Jill could see that Marilee was wearing blue mascara.

"Okay, I guess. It was a lot of fun. Do you fly?"

"I was learning, but I couldn't handle crosswind landings. It was just too hard for me." She scraped her matching green plastic bracelet against the counter.

"You stopped your lessons?"

"After I dumped four thousand dollars into it. My husband was so mad, but what can you do?"

Jill looked down.

"I'm sure you'll do fine, honey," Marilee encouraged.

Jill nodded and excused herself.

It was good to bike home. She needed to work out the charley horses from all that tension. Flying was so hard, but she couldn't help wanting to go back for the challenge. It was fun and hard, but possible. She could do this. Claire was a good teacher. She'd show her how to handle crosswind landings and everything else. Jill couldn't wait for her next lesson. She wanted to fly so bad it burned her. It'd crush her if Mom found out and put a stop to it. This was something she had to do no matter what. She reminded herself to be very careful so that Mom wouldn't find her flying books or any other evidence.

Weird thing was, even though she had nearly chewed off her lips, she wanted more stalls. Bring it on. In her heart, she felt like Lieutenant Dan in *Forrest Gump* shaking his fist at the storm and yelling for more. She was energized by the challenge, ready to take it on. Alive.

She had to find Nikka and tell her what she was doing and thank her for finding her dragonfly charm, which she now wore on her bracelet every day.

19 Wind Shear

"Nikka, do you know what this means?" Jill bobbed on her toes.

Nikka was tacking up flyers for a Fight Forest Industrialization Forum as she be-bopped around. She targeted another defenseless wood pole in the schoolyard and pierced it with tacks. Jill patted the pole's wound.

"It means the next time you land a plane you'll know how to land?" Nikka offered innocently.

"I'll be able to take Robbie for a ride. There's no way he won't notice a girl pilot. What's hotter than that?"

"Maybe you could try talking to him. That might work too. How'd you get your mom to agree?"

"If a piloting career doesn't work out, I could always go into forgery," Jill smirked.

"You didn't."

"What she doesn't know won't hurt her."

"But if you get caught, you'll be toast," Nikka said shaking her head in disbelief.

"How's she going to find out?"

"Hmm, let's see," Nikka put her hand on her hip. "The police are still looking for the runaway pilot who was with Old Vern. They're on the hunt. What if they find out it was you?"

"Thanks a lot," Jill said. "You always know how to put my feet back on the ground. God, I want to fly." Jill clutched her chest.

"Don't have an asthma attack." Nikka tacked a flyer up on a telephone pole near the parking lot. "I saw the photos in the paper, Jill. I'm worried about you. That plane was wrecked. Maybe your family is totally disaster prone. Maybe you should hold off. Let the curse lift, or something."

"Thanks. I knew I could count on you for support."

"I'm scared for you. Maybe this isn't supposed to be. Maybe these are signs you shouldn't ignore. No one ever got anything by deceiving themselves."

"How do you know? Have you ever tried it?" The wind blew some flyers across the lawn. Jill pounced after them and handed them to Nikka.

"What kind of friend would I be if I let you delude yourself?" Nikka asked.

"A very, very good one." Jill helped her flyer the bike rack, taping them to the side rails.

"I'm just worried about you, you know?" Nikka looked her in the eyes. "Please be careful. Slow down or something. What's your hurry to be a pilot? Cool your jets."

"Did my mom pay you?" Jill eyed her with the corner of her lips curling up. "Come back from the Dark Side." She mimicked holding up a light saber as she backed away.

"Come to the forum tonight," Nikka called as she moved to a tree but then decided not to tack it with a poster. "People are taking over the planet and ruining it. The forests are disappearing. You've got to come and help."

"That was the bell. I've gotta jet. I'll leave you to save Mother Earth from its treacherous human pestilence. 'The wretched hive of scum and villainy.'"

"If you're not part of the solution, you're part of the problem," Nikka called after her.

"Save the trees," Jill yelled back. "I believe in the trees!" She wrapped her arms around a tree. She couldn't resist teasing the tree-hugger, even though she admired Nikka for standing up for what she believed in, especially the beautiful forests that surrounded their town. But since Nikka took everything so seriously, she had to poke fun a little by circling her and chanting, "Trees, trees. I like trees."

"That's right." Nikka turned up her iPod and tuned her out. She put her nose between pieces of thick bark. "Smell it. Jeffrey pines smell like vanilla."

Jill just looked at her friend and laughed. What else could you say to a girl with her nose in a tree?

20 Constant Pressure

She didn't know how he had found out. She never expected her physics teacher, Mr. Brownstone, to know. Who could have told him?

From Jill's seat in the far back corner of the class, she was usually safe from Mr. Brownstone calling on her. Not today.

"Is it true, Jill?" Mr. Brownstone asked. "Rumor has it that you are learning to fly an airplane," he repeated.

"Yes." She tried to sink further under her desk as Mr. Brownstone walked down the aisle toward her. The little slab of wood made an insufficient hiding place. Small towns have no secrets. She didn't know how Mr. Brownstone found out about her lessons, but it made her nervous. Good thing Mom didn't usually answer the phone anymore. Jill would have to work harder to make sure she didn't.

"Tell us about it." Mr. Brownstone stood against the back wall. Jill turned around to face him. At least, she could pretend the rest of the class wasn't staring at her from behind. All she could see was Mr. Brownstone in front of her, self-consciously trying to cover his big beer belly with his overshirt. "So few of us have had the privilege of being up in an airplane. Tell us what it's like."

"It's like multitasking to the extreme. You have to talk on the radio while you're keeping the airplane going in a certain direction at a certain altitude and adjusting the engine to run with different types of air." Jill sat up straighter. It was, after all, her favorite subject. "You control the mixture of air and gas going into the engine depending on the air you are flying in."

"Excellent segue into today's topic. What kinds of air is Jill talking about?" he asked the class.

From the front row, Coby spoke up. "The air is less dense the higher you go up, so there's less atmospheric pressure."

"Exactly." Mr. Brownstone strolled down the aisle back to the front of the class. "Less air the higher you go until eventually you need oxygen supplements. Jill, you don't fly high enough to require supplemental oxygen, do you?"

"No. My Cessna tops out around ten thousand feet. Most people don't need extra oxygen that low in the daytime. But you do have to change the mix for the engine's best performance."

The beautiful girl with a long weave, Shaylin, in front of her, who had never so much as said two words to her before, asked, "What do you do as the plane goes higher?"

"I lean it, which means I adjust the engine's intake of gas. When the air is thinner, the engine runs better with less gas."

"Equalizing the ratio," Mr. Brownstone added. "How do you do that?"

"It's one of the billion knobs in the cockpit. You just turn it until the RPMs change."

The whole class looked at her with awe. She could almost hear the next question coming.

"How do you know how to handle all those things?" Neil, who sat across from her, asked.

Jill shrugged.

"A good instructor," Mr. Brownstone said. "Flying isn't something you can learn on your own. You're only as good as your training." Mr. Brownstone walked back to the front of the class. Jill breathed easier, but not for long. He turned toward her direction again.

"Jill," Mr. Brownstone said, "what else is different the higher you go in the atmosphere?"

"For one, the temperature. It's about two degrees Celsius cooler for every thousand feet you go higher."

"Does anyone know the name of that formula?"

"Lapse rate," Coby said.

Jill added, "The lapse rate helps you calculate your true airspeed." Jill saw Coby's expression — it was like he truly noticed her for the first time.

"What do you mean?" Shaylin asked. "There's different speeds in the air?"

"Yeah, it's pretty crazy," Jill said. "Your ground speed is how fast you are going across the ground. Your indicated airspeed is how fast the instrument says you're going, but this can be wrong because it doesn't take into account how temperature affects air which in turn affects how fast you can push against it."

Mr. Brownstone smiled that corny smile teachers get when their students seem engaged and interested. "And again, we are talking about air density."

Jill nodded. "Cold temps and air density affects performance of the engine."

The bell rang before she could launch into a discussion of how the wind affects airspeed as well.

As her classmates gathered their possessions to leave, Neil came up to her. Jill could see Shaylin out of the corner of her eye. She noticed Neil's attention was on Jill.

"Did you go up yesterday?" Neil asked. "The wind was nuts." Apparently Robbie wasn't the only one who thought a girl flying was cool. This was the first time Neil had ever talked to her, much less smiled at her the way he was smiling now.

"Yeah. There was a lot of turbulence coming off the north ridge but I went over the lake to practice power-off stalls and S-turns."

Four more guys, including Coby, gathered around. Jill could see the girls with Shaylin breathing jealousy out their nostrils.

"How much does it cost?" Neil asked.

"A hundred dollars an hour." Jill had never been surrounded by five guys asking her questions. For that matter, she had never been surrounded before by five guys.

"Yowza. You rich or something?" Neil asked.

"Not even. But if you look at it like college, even a private college costs way, way more than an education in flying."

"So this is your career thing?"

Jill didn't hesitate, "Yes."

"That's so cool. You're so lucky."

All the guys except Neil scrambled off to their next class. He lowered his voice, "Can you meet up with me after sixth? Parking lot. We can go to Brad's BBQ. I have a PT Cruiser."

"I know." Jill grabbed her backpack. She didn't know what to say. She didn't want to be rude but she really wasn't interested in Neil. He had earned every bit of his bad reputation. A user.

"Meet me at my Cruiser?" Neil asked.

"I can't. I have a lesson today." She bolted for the door and caught Mr. Brownstone smiling at her. Who knew just doing something she loved would make her the envy of the room? She paused to ask him how he knew she was learning to fly.

"Claire Cabello's a friend of mine," Mr. Brownstone answered.

"Small town," Jill responded. She wanted to ask him not to tell her mom. But parent-teacher meetings were a long way off, and she couldn't say that. Then he'd know she didn't have permission to fly.

"I'm proud of you, taking that on," Mr. Brownstone said.

Jill forgot about the danger of so many people knowing that she was flying and floated off to English with her head in the clouds.

21 Celestial Navigation

The suit Jill dug out of Mom's closet was a little wrinkled, but the navy blue, tailored cut definitely did the trick. She looked over eighteen. With a few more conservative touches, her hair up and Mom's pearl earrings, she was ready. Since she couldn't ride her bike in a suit, she had to tell Nikka about her plan. Because Jill had taken her sisters to Nikka's forest forum, Nikka was agreeable to anything.

When Jill heard a honk outside, she bolted to the door, almost forgetting to grab Dad's watch. Rushing in heels along the driveway, Jill twisted her ankle but caught herself as she stumbled to Nikka in her mom's Prius and got in.

"Oh my god." Nikka tried to stifle a laugh. "You look so … so … so …"

"Mature?"

"Like a grandma."

"I'll pass for eighteen, right?"

"You'll pass for over-the-hill." Nikka backed out of the driveway.

"Whatever. Just as long as I get the cash. I'm out of checks."

"You know you have to put money in your bank account, right? The checks don't magically make money appear."

"Really? Darn." Jill looked at herself in the visor mirror and fixed her smudged lipstick. "Whoopsie. That never stopped my mom. She bounces checks so much they ricochet out the mailbox."

Driving down the mountain, Nikka knew where she was going only too well, more familiar with the pawnshop outside the valley than she would have liked. Her mom occasionally hocked the Blu-Ray player when she was short on cash, in between selling paintings. Nikka thought it was crazy to keep buying it back at a much higher price than they sold it for, but her mom wasn't exactly good with money either.

"He won't ask for ID, will he?" Jill put on more eyeliner.

"I told you, just assume you don't need to mess with all that. Act like you're in a hurry and he's just the first pawnshop on your list. Bob is lazy. You'll do fine."

Jill took a deep breath. She had never wanted to be an actress, but this was important. If she blew it, she'd have no money for flying. Exchanging an item no longer needed by anyone for a career seemed like a good trade-off. It was time to prove she'd do anything to fly. She kissed the watch, wiped the lipstick off it and dropped it in her handbag. "Thanks, Daddy."

"You think he minds?" Nikka asked.

"I'm pretty sure if he needed to know what time it is where he is, he would have taken it with him." Jill peeked at it again. She wouldn't let herself be sentimental when her future was wrapped up in this thing from the past. She couldn't bring Dad back by stroking it three times and wishing. It wasn't a magic lamp. Maybe it would be good for her to let it go.

"It was his father's, though," Nikka said.

Jill felt a spike of guilt cut through her stomach. "Well, he doesn't need it either. And if you drive any slower, I won't need it. Jeez, could you get me there before I'm middle-aged?"

"If the shoe fits." Nikka laughed at Jill's outfit again.

When Nikka pulled up in the parking lot, Jill scanned the front of the pawnshop. It had big bars on the windows. Nice.

"Shady," Jill said.

"It's to keep people out when they sober up and realize they hocked their mother's antique diamond."

"Confessions of a starving artist's daughter."

"I've seen too much." Nikka feigned a hand to her forehead.

Jill nodded and got out of the car. Her heart raced as she walked inside. She sauntered past the display cases of jewelry and knives and walked up to Bob who looked nice enough, leaning on a stool and watching an old TV in the corner. He had his arms crossed in front of him and wore a soiled fishing hat. His gray beard had stains on the sides of his mouth, like a terrier.

"I'm interested in selling this platinum chronometer," Jill said, just like she had practiced. She set it down on the glass counter and braced herself, to look steady and sure. "It's worth ten thousand dollars and it has barely been used. It's practically new."

Bob took a long look at Jill, then at the watch.

"Who a what?" Bob asked. A foul odor escaped his mouth when he talked.

Jill could see the brown teeth he had hiding behind his beard. The man obviously had a fear of the dentist and probably the toothbrush too. It looked like it had been years since he brushed, maybe never. Reflexively, Jill took a step back. She realized it might seem rude, so she casually looked at the display case further away from Bob.

"Chronometer," Jill said. "It's a watch that keeps precise time. It's solid platinum."

Bob picked up the watch and inspected it closely. Jill wondered if he could smell his own breath bouncing off the watch.

"I have to get back to work right away, but I wanted to check out—"

"Two thousand."

Jill tried to keep her face expressionless. "Seven. It's worth ten."

"I'm not going higher than three. If you can get more for it than that, be my guest." He set the watch down and crossed his arms again.

"Okay, but could you hurry? My lunch break was over ten minutes ago."

Bob shuffled to a box under the counter and counted out the money. He offered it to her. Jill held her breath and tried not to grab the money too fast. She turned and thanked him.

"Not so fast."

In the middle of the store, Jill turned back and flashed a little smile. "Yes?"

"I need your name, address and ID. In case it's hot."

"It's not stolen. My husband died last year and I'm finally ready to let it go. You understand, don't you?"

"Cost you two hundred bucks to leave here without signing any paperwork."

Jill sucked in some fresh air before she walked back to the counter and handed Bob two one-hundred-dollar bills.

"Thank you kindly." Bob smiled. Jill almost passed out from the smell. She wanted to ask him what in the world would make a man that scared of a toothbrush but she left there as fast as she could with only one last glance at the watch. She whispered goodbye as she saw it go into a display case.

Back in the car, Jill flashed Nikka the pile of greenbacks.

"You did it!" Nikka made a little jumping up and down motion. "You juvenile delinquent!"

"We did it. Thanks for the coaching, but you didn't tell me about Bob's hygiene handicap."

"Oh, yeah. I forgot. Isn't it gross?" Nikka grimaced.

"What's wrong with him?"

"I don't know, but I bet it helps fend off the feds. If he were on your beat, wouldn't you skip checking up on him?"

"Police repellant stink mouth," Jill replied.

"You have nothing to worry about anyway. It wasn't stolen and I know your dad would approve if he were here."

"Tell that to my mom when she finds out. Which will be when I'm sixty-four, hopefully."

"You are so gonna get it when that woman wakes up and finds out what you've been up to."

"Shhh," Jill said. "Look! Money." Jill rubbed the stash against her cheek.

22 Level Out

When Jill parked her bike against the inside of the airport fence, she saw two men, sitting in lawn chairs on the side of the runway observing the planes come and go. She had often seen them sitting there with a cooler, watching the runway like it was homeplate on a baseball field. A line of planes waited at the end of the runway for their turn to take off. It was a good — busy — day to watch the flightline. Jill walked up to the spectators, taking notice of a curious little black leather book in the older man's hands.

"You're the girl taking lessons from Claire Cabello?" said the older man with white hair, thick round wire glasses and stubby legs sticking out of his shorts.

"Yes." Jill felt a surge rush through her. She was taking flight lessons. She was going to become a pilot. It was awesome being able to admit that. Strangers at the airport couldn't possibly tell Mom on her.

"I'm Burtie," he said.

The other one with short curly black hair graying at the temples shook Jill's hand. He wore a bright yellow and blue LA Lakers cap and jacket. "I'm Edmond. Claire's an excellent pilot," Edmond said. "She'll teach you up good."

"Do you fly?" Jill asked.

"Yep, nine years. I have a Warrior," Edmond said. He took off his Lakers jacket and hung it on the armrest.

Jill nodded even though she had no idea what that was. She looked down at the book in Burtie's hands.

"I've been flying just five," Burtie said, talking with his hands, even the one holding the book. He looked to be in his sixties. "I had to wait until the kids were out of the house. Wife's orders."

"Do you have a plane?" Jill asked.

"Sometimes," Burtie said.

Edmond laughed. "He means when his business partner brings it back here so he can take it out."

"When you have kids," Burtie said, "it takes a little longer to get your own toys."

They fell silent to watch a red-striped Cessna 172. It didn't take off like normal. It started going down the runway and then stuck its nose in the air too soon. It rushed down the runway with its nosewheel only off the ground.

"Even I could do better than that," Jill said. "He's popping a wheelie!"

"He's doing a soft-field takeoff. You have to practice that to get your license. FAA thinks we all should know how to take off from a muddy grass field."

"I haven't used that maneuver once," Edmond said.

"It's kind of fun, though," Burtie said. "You got to pop your nosewheel in the air and then hold it there until the bird flies. Hard to see to steer, though."

"It's hard enough to steer when you can see," Jill said.

"It gets easier," Edmond said.

"I gotta go. I have a lesson."

"Well, congratulations, Little Lady," Burtie said. "The first one didn't scare you away."

"No way." Jill pointed to the book in Burtie's hand. "What's that?"

"My logbook," he said. "Not a very big one, but I'm mighty proud of every single hour logged in it. You'll be getting one of these soon."

Jill waved goodbye as she ran over to Claire's hangar.

Thunder echoed off the north and south mountains, making a bowl of sound almost as loud as a Blue Angels fly-by. She wondered if a snow storm was coming in those lightning-jittery clouds. They flickered on and off like a faulty fluorescent light.

As Jill walked down the row of hangars leading to Claire's end, she peered in an open hangar along the way. It was Mr. Frib's. With as much time as she had spent at this end of the airport, saying goodbye to Dad before a business trip, or more recently, stalking Claire, she was in the habit of saying "hi" to Mr. Frib along the way.

Mr. Frib had often made empty promises to take her up flying one day. "One day, one day," he'd say to her and all the others drooling for a flight.

Admiring his shining new plane, Jill walked in the hangar and gawked at the marvel of modern flight.

"My, my, what do we have here: Claire's FlyGirl. Come look at my beaut," Mr. Frib offered as he walked around the high wing. "She's a new model." The gray ring of hair around his balding head was upset by the static from the wing grazing him. "Glass cockpit as well as the old-fashioned instruments. Do you want to see?" He held the door open. Jill came under the wing and looked into the cockpit. It looked shiny and new.

Excited with pride, Mr. Frib pointed out several instruments and rattled on about all their features. Jill was still trying to figure out what "glass cockpit" meant since the windshield looked like plastic, not glass. Tall and thin, Mr. Frib had to crouch under the wing as he rambled on. Getting concerned about the time, she had to find a way to interrupt him and politely leave. She looked at his striped business shirt and his middle-aged self-assuredness and tried to figure out how to cut him off.

"She's beautiful," Jill interjected. "I'm about to go fly too."

Mr. Frib backed out from under the wing and stood to his full height. "I'm going to rent her out to help pay for the loan. Do you think you'd be interested?"

"How much does it cost?" Jill asked.

"One twenty-five an hour. Very reasonable. You won't find a better deal around here."

"Yes, that sounds good." Jill moved toward the door. "I've got to go now."

"Sure, sure," Mr. Frib said as he set his keys on the shelf by the door. "I'm late myself." He rolled the hangar door on its tracks.

Jill continued two hangars down and slipped through Claire's door that was only cracked open a foot. It took her eyes a moment to adjust. Jack sat in the near dark, looking into a wing with a flashlight. When he heard Jill, he pulled his head out of the wing panel and said, "Flip on that light, would ya?"

Jill turned on the light. "Is Claire here?"

"She'll be back soon." Jack examined a grommet on the work table. "She had an important meeting. Must have run late."

Jill pulled out a wad of bills.

He eyed the dough. "Wowee. Girl Scouts make out like bandits nowadays—"

"I sold something." She set it down on the table next to him.

Holding two headsets, Claire marched into the hangar and saw the money. She spoke to Jill without looking at her or saying hello. "You can start the preflight using the checklist in the seat pocket."

"Hello to you, too," Jill thought. She went out to the plane, found the checklist and got down to business. She inspected the prop for nicks, which messed up the aerodynamics and could weaken the metal. She checked the wings to make sure the pins holding the ailerons were still tight. She gently kicked the tires to make sure they were inflated enough. When she was done with the list, she crawled in the cockpit and muddled with her shoulder harness. Her throat felt tight as she thought about sitting in the pilot's seat.

Every time she climbed in the pilot's seat, her heart did acrobatics above her tight lungs. Jill tried to calm herself as she strapped in, performing her usual fumbling show — dropping the seat belt onto the floor several times, obsessively smoothing her hair behind her headset, bumping her hands against the yoke whenever she reached up for the instrument panel. Finally, she was ready to start the engine. Claire jumped in and said, "Fire up."

Before cranking the propeller starter, Jill yelled out the window as loud as she could, "Jill!"

"What on earth are you doing?" Claire asked.

"You always yell 'Claire' out the window before you start her up."

Claire broke a smile. "No, I yell 'Clear,' as in, stay clear of the prop."

"Oh, that makes more sense." Jill hid her embarrassment and started the engine. She watched the engine gauges warm up and taxied down to the end of the runway. She followed the Before Takeoff checklist and performed its tasks.

"I have something for you," Claire said as she turned to the back baggage area and fumbled in her duffle bag.

Prior to lining up on the runway, Jill checked the sky carefully for approaching aircraft. It was clear.

"It's clear. Should I go?" Jill saw a little speck appear out near the other end of the airspace. She reminded herself to keep an eye on that plane since it might be flying in her direction.

Claire settled back in her seat with a little book in her hand. "A logbook for you. I put your student pilot's license in there."

"Cool! Thanks." Jill's chest fluttered with excitement. She had her own pilot's logbook.

Claire broadcast over the radio their intentions to depart, then said to Jill, "When you're ready, give 'er the gusto."

Jill turned up the gas. The plane charged forward, picking up speed and whining with wind. She pulled back on the control column and felt the ease of becoming airborne.

The world waned below them. The airport buildings shrank, but she didn't have time to see who was watching from the flightline. She kept her eyes on the airspeed and made sure it was right.

To level off, Jill pushed the control column in slowly and waited for the plane to catch up.

"You did it, FlyGirl," Claire said.

Jill stopped biting her lip long enough to smile. She let out a stale breath. She did it: her first takeoff all by herself, without someone's hands gently guiding the control column or being told how to do it. Jill took a few moments to celebrate this as she listened to the air traffic.

Flying was as amazing as she remembered. She felt herself lift as the plane did, in more ways than one. Her heart became ten tons lighter. It was so good to be back up.

"So," Claire said, "the forecast is a bit iffy today. Chance of rainstorms. Weather is something pilots always have to contend with. As they become more experienced, they make better decisions about when to fly or when to let the weather pass by. I'm usually a good mix of cautious and courageous. You have to develop good judgment. That takes practice."

Jill looked up at the sky. The dark clouds seemed miles off. "Looks good to me." Then again, the sky always looked good to her. "Lots of space up here."

Claire switched their radio frequencies. Jill listened to pilots talk to each other as she enjoyed flying the plane, getting used to handling all the directions a plane could go.

In mid-conversation, the voices of air traffic on the radio got dim. Claire tapped the voltmeter for the alternator, but the dial still sat on zero. The radio went off. All the electricity to the panel went out. Smoke filled the cockpit.

She pulled out the circuit breaker and opened a vent. The smoke cleared. She turned off the master switch, turned it back on and reset the circuit breaker. It didn't fix the problem — the radio display flickered on and off.

When the radio display lit back up, she spoke calmly over the radio. "SoCal Approach Control. This is Cessna Two Five Whiskey. I have an electrical problem. I have an electrical failure. Over." She hunched under the instrument panel and touched a bunch of wires, scooting under as much as she could to look for the problem, while Jill flew, constantly flicking over her eyes at Claire.

"Could be a wire's loose," Claire said.

"Electrical failure?" Jill asked. "We don't really need electricity, right?" The radio LCD went blank. "Oh."

Claire sat up and saw a fog bank had moved under them. Being unable to see the ground meant they didn't know where they were without using navigation instruments. Jill saw Claire's face tighten with tension. "Cessna Two Five Whiskey to SoCal. Come in, please," Claire said. The emotion was mounting in her voice as she called on the radio. "Come in, please." She tried to reach further under the panel as Jill continued to fly.

SoCal's answer was garbled on the radio. "Cessna... Over."

Claire dropped the wires and yanked some knobs. "SoCal," Claire said. "Cessna Two Five Whiskey. I have an alternator failure and the clouds have moved in. I am in between layers and I don't know where I am. I'm transmitting emergency. Can you identify my location and provide a vector to the nearest VFR airport?"

Jill realized Claire wasn't faking. They were in deep kimchee. She didn't know what transmitting an emergency signal meant but it sounded serious. She looked down and all across the land was a thick layer of clouds. A few mountain ridges peeked out the top of the layer but it was impossible to identify them. She had no idea what part of Southern California they were over.

SoCal's answer came garbled over the radio, "...copy that you have a problem..."

"SoCal, radio is failing," Claire said, "I'm going to turn it off for five minutes as I circle and look for any landmark." Claire shut off the radio and said under her breath, "Preferably not a mountain."

Everything fell silent except the drum of the engine. An eerie feeling of being lost and alone in the expansive sky crept over Jill and drained the feeling from her sweating hands. What if she never made it back? Mom would never forgive her.

They peered through the windshield and looked for a break in the dim gray soup below them.

"Early in your lessons and already an emergency," Claire said. "You're going to think flying is always like this. It's not. You're not going to know what to do when flying is boring. If you still want to fly after this…"

If Claire only knew she'd been in jeopardy before… But Old Vern dying during a flight was a big difference from having a mechanical problem up high in the sky. With the Old Vern flight, everything would have been fine if she had known how to land. Maybe Nikka was right about her family curse. Couldn't anything go right for her? "I wouldn't mind being on the ground right now," Jill said.

"I wouldn't mind seeing the ground." Claire kept searching out the windows.

23 Upslope Fog

It seemed like hours that they strained to see anything but fog beneath them as it got thicker and covered every bit of the earth. It was weird to look down and see only clouds. It was like the world had disappeared. The fog was upsetting Jill in so many ways. She liked having a course, not drifting in space. If flying was like this, then maybe she had been wrong about her dream. The thought was unsettling, rocking her off her foundation. If she didn't have her dream, what did she have? She really, really liked it better when she was rooted to flying. When she was sure. Clear. Clear vision, not this.

Claire turned the radio back on, but it was quiet. She went through the electrical failure procedure again.

Finally, a voice on the radio broke the tense silence. "SoCal approach," a man's voice said, "Piper 656, we have an aircraft with an electrical failure. I'd like an IFR clearance to go up on top of the clouds to assist. Over."

"Standby," the radio squawked.

"Someone's coming to help us," Claire said to Jill. She took over flying and banked into a shallow turn.

A layer of clouds moved in above them, dimming the light. The sky seemed unfriendly, bleak and gray. What was taking the Piper pilot so long?

Finally a voice pierced the static. "Piper 656. This is SoCal Approach. We have an IFR clearance. You're cleared to Paradise Vortac via the Big Bear departure. Climb to and maintain 12,000 feet." Jill wished she knew their secret language. She could only guess what was happening.

"They're coming to help us," Claire said to Jill. "Keep your eyes peeled for them."

"Peeled and browning." She felt sick. The clouds were

disorientating.

Looking down, there wasn't one hole punched out of the muck. Claire kept circling, trying to locate a break all the way down to the terra firma, perhaps big enough for her to fly through. Jill was glad she wasn't the pilot right now because the fear lodged in her throat felt like it was choking her. Luckily, Claire wasn't panicking.

"Man, do I want a cup of coffee!" Claire said.

"SoCal," the Piper pilot said over the radio. "This is Piper 656. Do you have a location on Cessna Two Five Whiskey?"

"Affirmative," SoCal said. "We had a skin paint with intermittent transponder. Suggest you take a heading of one-four-zero. Six miles to intercept."

Jill made her questioning eyebrows.

"It's good," Claire said. "Radar has us. They know where we are."

"Piper 656," Claire broadcast on the radio, "I'm getting low on fuel. Probably less than fifteen minutes left." The gas gauges bounced off empty.

"I'm almost there," the Piper pilot said. "Hang in there."

"Keep looking," Claire said to Jill.

"How will we keep from running into them?" Jill asked.

Claire was wearing a controlled expression. It reminded her of Dad's funeral where everyone donned stoic faces. How could she believe Dad was really gone when the world kept on spinning? A stab of terror pierced her chest as she realized that she could die right now. She knew it was too good to be true — learning to fly. Mom was right. Life really was too dangerous. People only pretended to have control…

The radio squawked. Nothing but noise. What was happening? What if the other plane busted out of the clouds and right into them?

They searched every speck in the sky for what might be an airplane climbing out of the cloud layer. Then, seemingly out of nowhere, a Piper Warrior appeared, heading toward them, dead on.

"You're at my nine o'clock position," the Piper pilot said on the radio before Claire found her voice.

"Got you in sight," Claire said. "Glad to see you." She let out a breath. She brought her plane parallel to the Piper and flew close to it.

"Follow the Pied Piper," a familiar voice said over the radio. Jack waved heartily from the Piper's copilot seat.

Claire looked surprised to see her father. "The weather changed so fast—" she said on the radio.

"No one could fly in this muck without instruments," Jack said.

"This old thing thought I needed a bigger challenge, I guess." Claire sounded embarrassed but happy her father had convinced someone to take him up on this rescue mission. "I swear this hunk of junk is out to get me." She hit the headliner with her fist.

"Stay close, we'll show you to the airport," the Piper pilot said. He leaned around Jack and waved. It was Edmond. It was easy to see his bright yellow and blue Lakers cap through the window.

"Lead the way," Claire said, sinking the plane into the fog a few feet away from the Piper, close enough to see the plane but far enough away that they wouldn't collide. The only thing visible in the murky sky was the other plane.

As the planes flew in formation, Jack kept waving. Jill laughed at his antics, warmed by his presence. She wanted to hug him.

The planes came out the bottom of the clouds and flew straight for the airport. The sun broke through a small hole and shined on the homeward-bound birds in final approach.

As soon as the planes wound down to a stop in front of the gas pumps, Jack jumped out and bear-hugged his daughter. "And so tell me again why flying is safer than driving?" Jack asked.

"Hey, roads are crowded with raging lunatics," Claire said. "Up there, it's only you and your training. Today was a good training day."

Jill threw chocks around the wheels.

Jack was still clutching at Claire's jacket. "I've decided you should be my assistant mechanic." He let go reluctantly.

"Yeah, right," Claire said as she gathered her headsets into her flight bag.

Jill glided to the pump and pulled the hose over to the wing, feeling proud Claire was still fearless. All was fine. Jill still had her dream, and it felt right. It belonged to her and she to it.

"Just another day at the office," Claire said.

"That scared me," Jack said.

"Come on," Claire said, "pilots are tortured by hours of boredom in the hopes for a few seconds of sheer terror." Claire winked at Jill as she stuck a credit card in the kiosk at the gas pump.

"She has a strange sense of fun." Jack threw his hands up and turned to Jill. "Are you okay?"

"I hope this still counts as a lesson," Jill said. When he hugged her, his aftershave reminded her of Dad. She had the childish urge to ask him for an ice cream cone, but he was in a hurry to get back to work on an engine overhaul.

As Jill entered the airport lobby, she saw Mom pacing like a caged lion in front of the windows. Baring teeth, Mom flared up and pawed at her, reclaiming her cub.

"Jillian Kate Townsend!" she roared as she laid a heavy hand on Jill's shoulder and led her to the front door.

"What are you doing here?" Jill asked, the shock of seeing Mom there was quickly replaced by embarrassment of seeing her in holey sweats.

"They called me." Mom pointed to the office clerk monitoring the radio. "The question is, what are you doing here? Let's go." She stormed out the lobby to the parking lot.

24 Cold Front

As Mom drove home, Jill was stressing to think of a way to diffuse the time bomb ticking next to her. It didn't help that they were driving past the graveyard.

"Mom, don't be mad."

"You blew it, pulling a stunt like that. That's it. You're not getting your driver's license. Ever!"

"You've been waiting to take that away from me. Are you happy you finally found an excuse?"

"That's enough, Jill."

"I didn't think you'd notice I was gone."

"Jill, I'm grieving." She said the word like it was a trophy. "I'm sorry if that means you don't get enough attention, but I lost my husband, my future, my everything, my—" Her anger turned to tears. She pulled the car over to the side of the road, next to the cemetery. Up the hill, the stone monuments went on forever. So many, passed. So many, nothing more than ash. Merely dust.

Jill's heart bottomed out as Mom sobbed.

"You don't know," Mom muttered between the retching sobs.

Jill slumped in her seat, sorry she upset her.

"I ruined your life," Mom said. "I ruined the family. I told him to hurry home—"

Jill froze. It had been a while since she had seen Mom cry in broad daylight, and never was it like this. She was literally disintegrating in front of her eyes.

"I told him to hurry home. It's my fault he died. I ruined your life. It's my fault. He was hurrying because of me... He wouldn't have gone off the overpass if he wasn't hurrying."

"Mom..." Jill touched her sobbing shoulder tentatively. What could she say to put Mom back together? They sat there for quite some time.

"Jill," Mom wiped up her tears and filled herself with sustaining oxygen, "if you could tell me why you want to risk your life, then, maybe… maybe I could understand…"

"It's not more risky than being in a car — 'they're death traps.' You say that and you still drive."

"Driving is unavoidable, and you know it. Flying is asking for trouble."

"What?" Jill couldn't speak for a moment and then she decided to tell Mom what only she knew. "You know, before Dad died, he told me something." Jill waited for Mom to soak in the words, to pay attention. She continued, "He told me he always wanted to be a pilot."

Mom looked at her dumbfounded.

"But he couldn't," Jill continued carefully. "He got too busy, supporting a family, he said. He said it was too late for him… to choose what he wanted to do. He said it wasn't fair to us."

"You're doing it for him?"

"No. For me," Jill said. "After I went up in a plane, I knew why he loved flying. I got it. Dad always did what he was supposed to and look where it got him." She motioned to the graveyard.

Mom let out a cry and then glazed over. Jill could have kicked herself. Why was she always saying the wrong thing? But then again, in the case of Mom, what wasn't the wrong thing? Jill buried her head in Mom's shoulder and cried with her.

25 Grounded

It was a bad idea to show up at the airport on a rainy day. In the lobby, Claire drained the coffeepot, scowling. She glanced at Jill as she stirred her coffee. Jill could tell right away that something was wrong. Claire's face brewed dark clouds.

"Your check bounced," Claire said. "It cost me twenty-five dollars. What were you thinking?"

"I'm sorry," Jill said. "I'll pay you back."

"You bet you will." Claire strode to the lobby doors. "Oh, and," she clutched the door, "the jig is up. Forging your mother's signature on a legal document is fraud. You're lucky I don't have time to prosecute you." She threw the door open. "Time to face reality, Little Girl." She stormed out.

Having witnessed the scene, Marilee behind the counter looked at Jill. She blinked her tarantula-thick eyelashes at her.

"Harsh," Jill said, with hope Marilee might be sympathetic.

"Taking a minor flying without permission is bad news. She could have lost her insurance, her business — everything."

"I'm almost seventeen," Jill said weakly.

"Why don't you come back in a couple of years?" Marilee returned to her paperwork, knocking her neon green and bright orange bangles on her desk.

Jill sunk into the window seat. This was a major mistake. Nothing could go her way now. Everyone was mad at her. Mom grounded her until adulthood. Claire hated her. She destroyed her one chance to fly. She tried, doing what she thought she had to do. She was wrong. She took matters into her own hands and it backfired. Now what was she going to do?

26 Obstruction Avoidance

After parking her bike in the Judsudeson yard, Jill tripped over a fairy on a stick. Nikka's mom's frontyard was a minefield. Ceramic toads and glass-winged statuettes jutted out of every corner. The chipmunk castles matched the house, with purple and pink facings. Whenever she wanted a good laugh, a view of the most interesting yard on the mountain was all she needed.

Nikka's mother, Tia, opened the door to their bright house that stood out among the other houses in Sugarloaf Mountain, which kept to earthy colors.

"Come in," Nikka's mother said as she wiped a paintbrush into a rag.

Jill walked past the hanging plants and large paintings stacked against the walls.

"Working on a new one, Tia?" Jill observed the latest on the easel. It was some loose-focus, colorful representation of a woman being zapped by a rainbow-colored cloud.

"Always." Tia led her down the hall. Her short white-blonde hair was tied up in a deep purple scarf that matched her eye shadow. "God likes it when we participate in the act of creation. He digs sharing his turf."

"Yeah, right. I forgot." Jill was sorry she asked. Tia was too out there to have a somber conversation with. When Jill was in a serious mood, like today, she avoided her as much as possible. She was more fun to talk to when Jill didn't have something heavy on her mind.

"Beauty comes—" Tia started.

"Is Nikka in her room?" Jill cut in.

She gave her a concerned smile and nodded, the same look she'd had since the funeral, like she was wondering if Jill was okay. Jill bolted away as if from a hot poker.

Nikka was rearranging the furniture in her room.

"Feng shui?" Jill asked.

"No," Nikka answered between grunts. Jill helped her move a mammoth dresser. "I thought of a more efficient arrangement."

Jill plopped down on Nikka's waterbed. As she floated on the bed, she looked at the mauve decor. "We should repaint the walls blue." She caused a hurricane by rocking on the bed. She still hadn't decided if she was going to tell Nikka about getting busted for flying. Nikka would definitely have an "I told you so" waiting. But she needed to talk about it.

Nikka put porcelain angels back on the dresser in specific destinations. "Grandma had a certain order for these," Nikka explained. "It's confusing to them if they aren't in the right place."

Jill ignored the subject of eccentric grandmothers and the placement of figurines. "Next you can help me move the fallen Heffalump in my house. I'm about to build a monument around her." Jill sat up on the rippling bed. "I don't know why she can't just let me fly—"

"You're obsessed." Nikka turned down her XM radio but still kept her hips going with the booming bass.

"Nikka," Jill ventured slowly, "I have to tell you something."

Nikka turned to face her and give her full attention.

"I'm not taking lessons anymore."

Nikka sat next to her. "What happened?"

After Jill explained, Nikka got up and finished her redesign by moving a lavender tasseled lamp to her night table without saying anything.

"Well?" Jill asked.

"Some dreams are too hard," Nikka said dismissively.

A spear of desperation pierced Jill's side. Maybe she had been fooling herself. If her bestfriend didn't think she could be a pilot, maybe she couldn't. She fell back on the bed and pretended she didn't hear Nikka's comment. At least she wasn't rubbing the failure in her face. "I only have a few minutes. I have to get home. Could I have your notes from English?"

Nikka pulled out a notebook from her bookbag. "Just take the whole thing. I already finished the assignment." She handed the notebook to Jill. "Come with me. I'm hungry."

"As usual," Jill said.

"Grazing takes all day."

"Yeah, that's why I let the moo-moos do it for me."

"Cow killer," Nikka said, but not seriously. She probably felt she had to take it easy on the meat-eater when her life was falling apart.

Jill followed Nikka to the front room. Crystally decorations of hearts and wings hung in the window and refracted the afternoon sun, catching Jill's attention. The prisms beamed color around the room. Humming, Tia lit a purple candle and sat at her sewing machine to stitch stars on a lavender quilt that had the same hues as her tie-dyed crinkle skirt and bandana halter top. Jill mused at the space cadet as Nikka set a bowl of unsalted, unbuttered popcorn on the living room table.

"Do you need help?" Nikka asked, referring the homework assignment.

Jill sunk onto the sofa and opened the notebook, scanning it quickly. Before Dad died, it was the other way around. But then, Jill had time to do homework. Now there was always something more pressing.

"Oh," Tia said. "Look what I found." She brought some photos to Jill. "This is a picture of me and your mom at prom."

Mom and Tia wore pastels and big hair.

"What was up with puffy dresses and poofy hair in the eighties?" Jill asked.

Nikka sat next to Jill. "How could anyone ever think that looked good?" she asked between chomps of dry popcorn.

"This is your parents' wedding," Tia said as she held out another photo. "She had your father's life planned before he knew what hit him."

"Sounds familiar." Jill noticed the happy tears in his eyes.

"They were off and married before she graduated from college." Tia passed the photo to her.

"She told me she thought she'd never need a degree since she got her MRS degree," Jill said. "Her whole world was Dad and now he's gone."

"He had a way of bringing her out. She let her hair down around him. With her glow, you could see a thousand light years ahead. They had such a bright future." Tia showed a photo of Mom wearing red vinyl pants when she was younger. "Your father used to call her Fancy Pants. She wore those things for a whole year of parties, it seems."

"My mother wore those?" Jill asked.

"I didn't know," Nikka said. "How come we were never told

about the bowling ball pants?" The tight red vinyl sparkled like a bowling bowl.

Jill took a closer look. "There's obviously a side to Fancy Pants I've never seen. You'd think a woman who wore red vinyl pants would understand the need to find your own path. I don't know why she can't let me be me. She's not doing so hot herself."

"Why don't you ask her?" Tia said. "Consider this, Jill," she laid a motherly hand on her shoulder, "compassion is knowing someone's screwing up, making the wrong choice, but loving them anyway."

Jill's stomach dropped to the floor. "Why do I always have to be the grown up? She's the mother."

"I didn't say it was fair. Compassion doesn't care about what's fair."

Jill lowered her head. She felt torn between empathy for Mom and screaming, "what about me?" Why did Jill's life have to suffer because Mom wanted it that way?

"I know it's hard." Tia squeezed her shoulders in a quick hug and then returned to sit at her sewing machine. "You can keep that photo if you want."

Jill pocketed the photo and looked at her wrist, but there was nothing there. "What time is it?" She was more than ready to split.

"Time to go." Nikka grabbed her backpack and headed for the door. "I'm giving Jill a ride home."

"May the Light guide your path," Tia said as she blew a kiss at her daughter. Nikka rolled her eyes. Jill stopped laughing when she tripped over a yard troll outside the front door.

* * *

"This is your captain speaking," Nikka said on the phone. "You must go to college weekend with me."

Jill switched her cell to her other ear and answered Nikka, "I'm sorry."

Two weeks had passed since Jill got busted and she hadn't left the house except for school.

"It's such a bummer you can't go," Nikka said. "She can't ground you forever."

Jill looked out her bedroom window at the dark clouds rolling down the south mountain ridge. Boding thunder echoed across the valley. "Just till I'm eighteen. Which might as well be forever. I'll suffocate before then."

"I'll take notes. I'll tell you everything." Nikka's voice was making a good effort at trying to sound positive, but Jill knew how disappointed Nikka was that she wasn't allowed to join her for college weekend.

They had planned which dorm they would stay in, how to find the art department for Nikka and the physics department for Jill. They googled all the cool cafes and galleries in the area. Now Nikka would have to go alone. "I'll be able to tell if this is your college destiny. And don't worry, I'll ask how many students pass the flight program."

Jill lay back in her bed and looked up at the blue ceiling. "I'm not sure I'm even going to college now, Nikka. Everything's messed up."

Suddenly, Jill heard screaming. She bolted up, dropped the phone and ran down the hall. It was Bre. She was screaming bloody murder. Jill found her lying on the floor next to the dining room table.

"Bre, baby, what's wrong?" Jill tried to scoop her up in her arms but Bre shot away, screaming, holding her left arm. Her pajamas were ripped. Mom rushed in.

"What happened?" Mom asked.

"I don't know," Jill said over the screaming. Each yelp tore at Jill's heart. Her baby sister was in pain and she didn't know why.

"Weren't you watching her?" Mom demanded.

"I put her to bed a few minutes ago. She fell asleep when I was reading her Peter Pan. She was fine." Jill tried to touch her again and Bre screamed louder. Jill looked at the hallway and saw Kelly creep down to the end and stop, looking scared. "Do you know what happened?"

Kelly shook her head. Trying to hide, she pulled her long hair in front of her face, which was contorted into a pre-sob.

"What's wrong, baby?" Mom asked Bre as she tried to exam the arm she was clutching. Mom lifted the flap of pajama near her shoulder.

"I fly," Bre sobbed.

Jill noticed a stack of books next to the counter. "I think she was trying to fly. Off the counter."

Mom scowled at Jill.

"Like Peter Pan," Jill added weakly.

Mom unbuttoned the top of Bre's pajamas and gasped.

Jill saw her collarbone budging in a knot between her shoulder and her neck. She felt like she was going to pass out. Instead, she ran for the car keys and gave them to Mom.

27 Graveyard Spin

Hours later, Jill still held Kelly though her arms felt like they were going to fall off. She carried her over to the emergency room counter and set her on it. Kelly clung to her neck. Jill pat her back rhythmically. At seven, she was too big to be held, but Jill couldn't get her to let go.

"Do you know how much longer?" Jill asked the nurse behind the counter.

"There's a problem with your insurance," the nurse said. "We called to pre-authorize and they said your family's insurance was cancelled due to non-payment."

"So?" Jill could hear Bre crying in the examination room even though Mom was holding her.

"Your family is going to need to pay. Do you have a credit card?"

Jill felt like the nurse hit her in the stomach. She wished Dad was here. Bre was balling and they didn't have the money to fix her.

"If not," the nurse continued, "we can set up a payment plan. Have your mom fill this out." She shoved a stack of papers at her.

Five hours later, back from the ER, Jill watched Bre sleep in her bed. Mom stepped in too. "They set it back in place but she needs surgery," Mom said. "We don't have that kind of money."

A thunderstorm of desperation crackled into Jill's mind. She looked at the closet. She wanted to crawl in it.

"Come here." Mom walked down the hall to the living room. She collapsed in a chair. Jill stood next to the Stardust urn on the mantle. Mom didn't say anything. She stared at the floor.

"I'm sorry, Mom." Jill shuffled toward the hallway.

"You're a strong girl, Jill. I'm sorry I haven't been there for you. I'm sorry I ruined everything for us."

She wanted Mom to talk, but she didn't want her to start on this again. Then, she remembered what Tia said and sighed. Jill sat tentatively on the edge of the couch. "Isn't life for making mistakes? Isn't that how we learn? I mean if we did it perfectly, we wouldn't learn anything." She scooted closer and put her hand on Mom's.

"You remind me of myself," Mom said, "when I was younger. Full of so much hope…"

"What happened to you, Fancy Pants?"

Mom looked up. "Where did you hear that nickname? Your father used to call me that."

Jill pulled the photo out of the drawer in the table. Mom smiled when she saw it.

"What happened to you?" Jill asked.

Mom's eyes softened. "I was following a blueprint, I guess. I had plans for family… financial security — all the milestones. I was in a race to get everything in order. To tell you the truth, Jill, I was trying to get us to look like a normal family so someone would say I was okay. Do you understand?"

Jill nodded uncertainly. "You're okay, Mom. Even without Dad here, you're okay."

"I'm sorry." She looked like she's going to start crying again. "I'm having trouble believing I'll never get another chance. What I wouldn't do for one more day to be with your father."

Jill put her arm around her. "You're the one who was always telling us that there's life after death. What about all that eternal soul stuff? Don't you believe what the preacher says?"

"I just miss him."

"So do I."

"How are we going to afford Bre's surgery?"

"Hang on a minute." Jill left the room and returned a moment later, holding the rest of her cash.

Mom looked at her with apprehension. "Where did you get that?"

"You can use this money for Bre. See, everything will be okay. I had plans for it, but—"

"Where did you get that wad of money?"

"I sold Dad's chronometer."

"Jillian Kate Townsend, you did what?" Her nostrils flared.

"I was going to use it to pay for flight lessons, but Bre needs it more."

"You sold your father's watch?" Mom repeated.

"He would have wanted it. He'd say there are plenty of things we can get sentimental about that don't cost thousands of dollars. He was very practical. You made him that way—" She stopped when she saw Mom's face fall. "It's a good thing, too, because look at all he left us." Jill pointed to the airy log cabin.

"Don't you ever sell anything again without telling me first. Do you hear me?"

"Loud and clear. Roger that. Just be glad I didn't sell your wedding ring."

Mom looked down at her left hand.

"Just kidding." Jill was relieved to see the frown disappear from Mom's face. She watched her take a deep breath and ease back into her chair. "You don't really think I'd do that, do you?"

"You wouldn't dare. Jillian Kate, you will not sell anything else from this house, do you hear?" Mom looked at the money and her face lifted.

"Yes, okay." Jill felt like the room was getting lighter. "Unless of course you have something around here worth a plane." She smiled at her exasperated mother. She was pretty sure Dad was smiling too. She decided to stop while she was ahead and not bring up what was really on her mind: how to get back up in the sky.

28 Wing Span

It was the Dawn of the Dead. Mom was up and even dressed, reading on the couch. A fire crackled below the urn on the mantle. Jill moved the Stardust urn to the coffeetable, pulled out a little pickling jar from a drawer and set it next to the urn.

"I like your non-repose," Jill said.

Mom kept reading her book. "Did you do what I asked?"

"I'm doing it now. Is it okay if I do this here?"

Mom nodded.

Jill opened up the urn and scooped some of Dad's ash into the pickling jar. Mom had asked her to send Aunt Pam a To-Go package for her mantle. Aunt Pam was ready to have a memorial too, since there was no gravestone to visit.

"I really am glad to see you up," Jill said as she put the urn back in its spot.

Mom still didn't look away from her book. "Don't get used to it. I'm just trying it out to see if I remember how." She shifted in her chair. "Yep, hasn't changed much. The world is pretty much the way I left it."

"You shouldn't say that. Bre and Kelly need you..." Mom's eyes didn't leave the book in her hands, although they did halt their movement across the page. Jill finished what she was doing, stood up and pulled on Mom's hands. "Get up, Fancy Pants. You have to babysit for me today. I've gotta go look for a job."

"What?"

"I've gotta pay for flight lessons somehow. I thought I'd try the old-fashioned way—"

"You think you'll ever step foot in a plane again?" Mom's nostrils were doing the flaring thing again. Didn't rhinos do that before charging?

"I'll be eighteen in less than two years. You can't stop me then.

It will take me that long anyway to earn enough to pay—"

"Why, Jill, why?" Mom fell back into the couch. "Why can't you let it go?"

"I love flying, Mom. You can't take that away from me. It's in my bones. They're part bird. I was meant to fly. I must be or I wouldn't love it so much." Jill grabbed her jacket and backpack and headed for the door. "I'm not grounded from working, am I?" Jill waited for Mom to respond.

Mom picked up her book. "Be home in time to make dinner."

After applying to seven minimum-wage jobs, Jill stopped by the airport on the way home. Sitting in his folding chair at the flightline, Burtie greeted her. He was watching the runway alone today.

"Do you want a soda?" He opened the ice chest next to his chair.

Jill shook her head. "Where's Edmond?" She sat in the empty chair next to Burtie.

"He's being interviewed by the police," Burtie said as he lifted a soda from its resting place on his big belly to his mouth. "They seem to think two old fellers watching the world go by might know something about Old Vern's demise."

Jill's stomach lurched. "He died of natural causes, didn't he?"

"Why, sure, but it's very strange his student would run off like that. They tracked down the student who was scheduled to fly with him and he said he was late to his lesson and never saw Vern. No one knows yet who was flying with him. Must have been a last minute change in the schedule that Vern didn't have a chance to write down. So the police are asking for the names of all the student pilots we can think of."

Realizing she was holding her breath, Jill let it out and tried to look calm. "Did you tell them about me?"

"I told them you were a student of Claire's." Burtie rested the soda can back on the shelf his protruding belly made. "You've never flown with Old Vern, have you? I didn't think—"

"No, oh no," Jill lied quickly. "No, I was just wondering…"

Burtie sized up Jill, then returned his gaze to the runway. A twin-engine airplane was taking off.

Jill quickly thought of a red herring to throw out there, in case Burtie was sensing she had something to hide. "What about the CAP cadets?"

"As far as I know, there haven't been any student pilots in our local chapter for quite a while since there's no trainer plane available for them. But you may be right. Vern was the flight instructor on record for the cadets should they ever raise enough money to get the flight training program going."

"I have to go." Jill stood up so quickly her seat folded up and fell to the ground.

Burtie eyed her. "You wouldn't happen to know anything about Old Vern's last flight into the Great Unknown, would you?"

Jill couldn't stand the way Burtie was looking at her — expectantly, maybe even suspiciously. "No, sorry." She excused herself and rode her bike home so fast, the wind made her eyes water long streamers.

29 Warm Front

The CAP lieutenant, Mr. Michaels, stood at the front of the airport lobby, demonstrating aerodynamics around a small toy plane to some cadets. Jill was happy the meeting hadn't started yet. She was running late since she had to wait for Mom to be distracted by her sisters' squeals in the bathtub before she could sneak out.

Spotting Robbie in the back next to the platter of waxy cookies, Jill headed to him. A pretty blonde girl, wearing a CAP uniform, was talking to him. Jill knew who she was, Chelsea, but didn't know much about her other than she was scoping Robbie. In fact, gossip had it that Chelsea was hoping Robbie would ask her to their senior prom. Jealousy verging on panic seized Jill. She butted in.

"Hey." Jill stood between them. Chelsea's face nearly rolled into a slight snarl when she saw Jill. "I'm thinking of joining CAP. Do you get to fly?"

"We get to go on S and R missions," Robbie said. He smiled when Jill made an expression like she didn't understand, and explained, "Search and Rescue. But I have yet to get behind the wheel. We don't have a trainer plane up here. Other squadrons do, so I keep hoping they'll share."

When he smiled again, electricity shot through her as she became lost in his perfect smile, perfect teeth, perfect lips.

"Good luck with that," Chelsea said as she flipped her long gorgeous hair behind her shoulder. "I hear the Long Beach squadron has a two-year waiting list just for the intro lesson."

"Really?" Jill felt herself go on a five-alarm firehouse alert as Robbie was now looking at Chelsea instead of her. She had to do something. "I've already had lessons. I can fly," she announced proudly.

"What? No way." Robbie said. His eyes sparkled. "With who?

Where?"

"Here. With ol—" Jill stopped herself. She almost said Old Vern. What a dunce. She couldn't say Claire considering how badly that went. Chelsea might have heard of the scandal or something. She'd be only too happy to bring it up and reveal that Jill forged permission and bounced checks. "My dad." That should be a safe answer. No one questioned her about her dad. It was a forbidden subject to most people.

"Is that how he died?" Chelsea asked with not a hint of sympathy in her voice.

Jill stared at her. No, she didn't. No, she didn't.

Robbie answered. "No, of course not, Chels."

Surprised, Jill looked at Robbie. He knew how Dad died? Her heart melted. It was in the papers but, obviously, not everyone paid attention to the news. Robbie must have seen her eyes get slightly wet, because he quickly changed the subject.

"Have you soloed?" he asked.

Jill thought of the time Claire was unconscious in the pilot's seat and the time Vern, well... "Yes," she said.

"Cool. That must be so awesome alone up in the sky."

"It is."

"Weren't you scared?" Chelsea was trying to reinsert herself back into the conversation.

"Maybe the first time, but then you get used to it."

"Oh man," Robbie was nearly melting over the thought of soloing. "Did you get to do stalls? When you were taking lessons?"

"Oh, yeah. Easy — unless of course your instructor happens to be snoozing and you accidentally go into clouds."

"You went into the clouds?"

"Just a little. Ooopsie." Jill was wondering why she was saying words like "Ooopsie." Was this flirting? Were childish words making her more attractive? Robbie's attention was fully on her and she could see in her peripheral vision that Chelsea was none too happy about it.

"That's how a lot of VFR pilots go down," Robbie said.

"I know. Believe me, I know. It was crazy." The way he looked at her fried her brain. Before she knew it, she was talking crazy. "I can show you our plane. My dad — he had a plane that's just sitting around now."

"Yeah, sure."

"Tomorrow during lunch break. The back corner of the East T-hangars."

Just then, Mr. Michaels interrupted as he finished a phone call.

"We have a mission, Cadets." Mr. Michaels gathered everyone to the front of the lobby near him. "Search and Rescue. Two hikers are lost somewhere in the north mountains. They were supposed to be in last night from the PCT. If any of you have been on the Pacific Crest Trail, you know how confusing it is this time of year with all the erosion offshoots." He looked at his watch.

"We have to hurry before the sun goes down. A CAP plane is already headed our way from Fullerton. They can take three more sets of eyes." He looked down at a clipboard. "Robbie, Trevor and Chelsea. Your turn." Robbie and Trevor high-fived each other and then pounded fists. "Get over to the CAP hangar pronto. Grab your gear and wait at the fuel pit. They should be landing in ten. Move it out, Cadets. Go."

Robbie bolted with Chelsea at his heels. Trevor downed the rest of his energy drink and sprinted a second later.

Without Robbie there, Jill left the meeting to sneak back home to her room before Mom noticed she was gone.

* * *

Time crept slowly as Jill watched the clock in World History, waiting for lunch break. Even though she had little hope that Robbie would actually meet her at the airport, the minute the bell rang, she rocketed out of class and to her bike. With the hikers still missing in the forest, another team would be going out. It wouldn't be Robbie's turn to join CAP searchers today. She wished she could go with them, even as a passenger. Anything to get back in the sky...

The vehicle gate at the north side of the airport was stuck open. Biking through it, she looked at the windsock. Not too bad. It was halfway inflated, meaning the wind was about eight knots. She turned down the row of East T-hangars and saw Claire's plane was gone from the tie-down spot in front and the hangar was closed. She hadn't counted on that. Claire didn't normally fly on Wednesdays. *Crap, just my luck.*

Now how would she show Claire's plane to Robbie? Maybe Claire would return the plane in time and leave before Robbie showed up. Yeah, right.

Jill leaned against Claire's hangar and watched Mr. Frib push his new Cessna into his hangar across the way.

After he got the plane tucked in his hangar, he dropped the keys to his plane on a shelf next to the entrance. She knew what was next in his routine. He'd finish putting his plane to bed by putting a cover over the instrument panel.

Jill searched the row of hangars and then the perimeter fence. She thought she saw Robbie way at the other end of the airfield, walking around the outside of the fence. He was coming. And she didn't have a plane to impress him with. How was she going to explain this to him? She couldn't tell him she liked him so much that she lied about Dad having a plane. What a loser.

Panic reached up Jill's throat, choking her with bile. She had to think of something quick. She looked back at Mr. Frib's plane and remembered all those empty promises he made to take her up flying one day. "One day, one day," he'd say. Yeah, right.

"One day" was today.

She saw Robbie getting closer, walking next to the fence.

Jill looked back at Mr. Frib. This was her chance. As he turned and reached in the back of his plane, Jill acted fast before she could think about what she was doing. She walked in his hangar ten inches, grabbed the keys, stuffed them in her pants pocket and kept walking past the hangar.

Mr. Frib looked up. Jill's heart stopped, but she played it off with a smile and wave. Mr. Frib waved back.

As Jill tried to look casual tying her shoes, waiting for Mr. Frib to put the big padlock on his hangar and leave, she saw Robbie making his way down the row. She called to him.

"Hey." Jill tried to wrangle messy strands of hair behind her ear.

"Hey." Robbie sauntered to her spot and looked her in the eyes.

She grabbed the wall and steadied herself. The way he looked her right in the eyes, so comfortable, as if he walked into any situation calm and easy, made her freeze. She lost the uniquely human skill of speech. Her brain locked up.

Too many things were colliding through her head, like how she had managed to get the attention of the hottest senior in school and very likely the entire universe, or how his lips were perfect and relaxed into a slight smile and his eyes were deeply piercing into her soul, or how

Nikka was going to cross a river and drown when she heard the news that Robbie Magnor was talking to her — alone!

Forming one suitable sentence was impossible. "I'm gonna go flying. You wanna come?" She had no idea what she was doing or why that popped out of her mouth. His deep brown eyes must have made her temporarily insane every time she caught a glimpse of them. And now they were incredible, full of life.

"You're going flying?" Robbie's eyes lit up.

"Yeah, sure. I was just checking out the weather, looking at the windsock." She glanced over at the orange flag flopping in the breeze. "Looks good. No crosswind or nothing."

"Where you going?"

She had no idea. What was she doing? She was in it now.

When she didn't answer, he offered, "Vegas?"

Jill snapped herself out of it. "Just to Palm Springs. It's about an hour flight there and back. I'll be back before sixth period." She forced her legs to move toward Mr. Frib's hangar. As she looked all around to make sure Mr. Frib was long gone, her heart was racing. Was she really going to do this? She glanced at Robbie. Eagerness lit up his face. She had him.

Her hands faltered as she tried to put the key into the padlock on the hangar door. Finally, she got the lock off and pushed the heavy door on its tracks. The shiny plane looked good with its perfect paint job, mostly bright white with a deep maroon stripe down the fuselage. It nearly took her breath away. She almost hugged its nose but remembered Robbie was with her. She didn't have to spread out all her weird just yet. Nikka was about the only person who could handle Jill in all her glory. Best to keep it on the down-low until the boy became hooked by her talent and intellect. Jill laughed at herself. Somebody had to…

"This plane is smokin.'" Robbie was entranced by the little two-seater. "Whoa," he circled the plane, "this is your family's? You are so lucky! When did you get your pilot's license?"

"I've been flying since forever. We fly to the outback every summer." Jill looked at the two seats side by side and added, "My father and I, we'd visit grandma in Montana."

"That's cool. I'd kill to fly."

"Let's go, then." Jill climbed in the pilot's seat. Without hesitation, Robbie took the right seat. While looking at the checklist hanging on the side panel, she flipped a red switch. "Master switch on." She stuck the key in the ignition, turned it and pushed the button labeled "start."

The propeller turned and roared to life. The plane shook, papers flew around the hangar and the noise echoed deafening loud in the small garage-like space. The plane jumped forward. Jill jammed her feet on the pedals and the plane jerked to a stop.

Jill cleared her throat. "The brakes work. Just checking."

She saw papers flying around the hangar and realized why no one starts their plane inside a hangar. It looked like a hurricane had hit. Releasing the brake pedals, she let the plane roll out of the hangar and to the taxiway toward the end of the runway fast, in case anyone happened to be watching. Regulars at the airport would know she wasn't supposed to be in Mr. Frib's plane. She hadn't seen Burtie and Edmond today, but just in case, she pushed the throttle in a little more and the plane picked up speed.

She nearly veered off the taxiway, swerving back and forth as she tried to control the plane and get it to stay on the marked path. She didn't dare look at Robbie to see what he thought of her crazy driving. He didn't know how hard it was to steer with your feet, especially going fast.

Finally she made it to the end and paused for a minute to look at the sky. No traffic coming in to land.

"You ready?" She had to talk loudly to be heard over the engine noise.

Robbie's excited face said it all. "Launch when ready, Captain."

Jill pulled the plane out on the runway and lined up on the center line. She pushed the throttle all the way in and the plane zoomed down the runway. It was way louder without a headset.

She wasn't sure when to pull up on the yoke to get airborne, but when the wheels started bouncing on the asphalt, she figured it was time.

She yanked back on the yoke and they fell against their seats. She corrected by releasing some back pressure on the control column. She gave Robbie a cocky smile so he'd think she meant to do that.

"Show off," he said with a big smile.

She gently turned the plane toward the gap in the mountains that led to the desert beyond.

"You wanna try?" She took her hands off the yoke.

Robbie grabbed the yoke on his side, the control column in front of him. The plane dipped down.

"Pull up a little," she instructed. "You got it."

"Cool." He was so hooked. She had never seen his smile so wide. She watched him a minute then realized she was staring. He caught her eye and smiled.

She looked away, shy from the intensity of his eyes. Glancing down, she saw her house pass by. No sign of life at home. Mom would totally kill her if she knew what she was doing right now. Maybe she could keep going, fly to Mexico and never come back. That would show Mom. What was that saying she read in her history book? "Give me liberty or give me death." She could relate. How long could she stay locked up and grounded before she went nutty? Who cares? She was out of there. If Robbie wanted, she would keep on flying to the end of the horizon. She was free.

Soon they were over the desert. Jill noticed all the rocks, cactus and dirt looked the same for miles and miles. Ut-oh. Which way was Palm Springs? She peered out the windshield and side windows, starting to panic. If she couldn't find her way to Palm Springs, she didn't know where there was another airport to land at.

"Is something wrong?" Robbie asked.

"To be honest, I've misplaced Palm Springs."

"Why don't you turn the GPS on?"

Jill looked blankly at Robbie. "Oh, yeah, right." She looked at the instrument panel and didn't see anything that looked like a digital map. "Why don't you do it while I fly?"

Robbie pushed a button on a square device mounted in the middle of the panel. "We use a Garmin when we do S and R, but this shouldn't be too different. Here it is." He punched buttons. "Go right."

Jill looked at the GPS. Sure enough, it showed a little plane in the middle of a moving map with Palm Springs to the right. She started a gentle turn.

"Check this out." Robbie took over the yoke and sent the plane in a sharp dive and turn.

Jill released her grip, letting Robbie act as Pilot In Command. She fell against the side window. "I bet we're pulling five Gs."

"You can take it?" Robbie handed her a barf bag and rolled hard into another turn. His biceps were flexing as he pulled the yoke. Again, he caught her looking and smiled.

She threw the barf bag behind her. "'Course. G-pulling should be a sport, like disc-throwing or something."

The G-forces eased up as he leveled the wings and the roller-coaster feeling dwindled in her stomach. She looked out the window to her left at a man, the size of a bee, digging a hole in his backyard.

At one thousand feet above the desert town of Landers, she could see what people were doing in their fenced yards as they whizzed by at 120 miles per hour. This was so awesome. Flying a plane. With the hottest guy in school! Wait till she told Nikka. There's no way she'd believe her. Jill wished she had a camera to immortalize this moment, only the best moment of her life.

"That's Joshua Tree National Park." Robbie pointed ahead. "I went camping there and rock climbing near Skull Rock. I think that's it over there."

Jill wished he'd take her camping there.

Suddenly the engine started making weird noises. The propeller sputtered, and awful, explosive, choking noises got louder. Her throat tightened.

"Um," Robbie said, "do these gas gauges work?"

Jill looked at the two gauges that both read empty. She stifled a gasp.

"Cuz if they do," Robbie continued, "that's not so good."

Jill's stomach jumped out her throat. Gas! Mr. Frib flew the plane and didn't refill it. How dumb could she be? She forgot about gas! The engine was quitting. They were going down. Ain't nothing you can do when you're out of gas. Hello.

She had been in such a hurry and distracted by Robbie, she hadn't even thought about the most important thing. Jill looked down at the desert floor clipping by.

Outside Yucca Valley, cactus, rocks and sage brush spotted the dirt. She held the plane level as they sank helplessly. The engine sputtered out and the prop stopped windmilling. This thing was a glider now.

She could probably glide it down but landing was tricky. Pelting the ground this fast required a clear spot to touch down. Most likely, they would crash into something.

No open, flat strips of land were anywhere around them for miles. They were screwed. Boulders and Joshua trees jutted up everywhere. The rolling hillsides were cracked into channels of erosion and gullies. If they hit one of those, they'd flip over. Hard.

"Robbie, I'm so sorry. I think we must have had a leak or something. The tanks were full." Yesterday, she almost added.

"You can land out here, right?"

"Yeah, sure." They were going to die. She was going to die at sixteen with Robbie Magnor next to her. She almost pulled Robbie into a kiss. This was her last chance. She was going to die without ever being kissed. There were no words for what kind of Loser with a capital "L" she was.

Cool-headed, Robbie looked nervous but not terrified as he braced himself for an off-field landing. Should she tell him they were going to die? She didn't see any safe spots ahead to touch down.

The ground coming up grabbed her attention. Sharp rocks rushed by, raking closer. In seconds, it was all going to be over.

Cactus ripped past as Jill tried to pull up on the yoke, but the plane only sank more, stalling out. If she lived through the next second, it wasn't going to be pretty.

Jill wanted to close her eyes and brace herself but she didn't because she had to see it through. She concentrated hard on keeping the wings level and not stalling this close to the ground — no matter how much she wanted to tug back on the yoke, she knew it wouldn't make the plane climb. It would only make them crash head first, loping over the stalled wing.

Panting, petrified, she held it level with all her strength.

With a crunching metal thud, they hit the ground hard.

The last thing Jill remembered was hitting a boulder, the landing gear collapsing and the prop bending like a pretzel.

And pain.

Great, big pain.

30 Squall Line

"**A**re you okay?" Robbie's voice came from somewhere around her.

Was she dead? She didn't think she could move. Suddenly, she could see. Her eyes were open and she was looking at blood. Robbie's blood. His forehead had a gash that was flowing so much dark red blood that Jill gagged and threw up. When she stopped, she found herself sitting next to a rock. The plane was two feet away.

"We need to move away from the plane," Robbie said.

Jill looked at the pieces of metal. What plane? Gas puddled next to the broken-off wings.

"Are you okay?" she asked.

"I'm fine."

She looked at the wreckage. "I'm in so much trouble."

"It wasn't your fault."

Jill tore her sleeve off and pressed it against Robbie's forehead.

"Thanks." He held it harder to stop the bleeding. "We really need to move. Can you walk?"

She didn't know. She tried standing up and her ankle collapsed. Robbie caught her. The pain shot up her leg like a knife. They hobbled away from the wreck and sat on a rock. Jill looked at Robbie's arm. It was bleeding too.

"I'm so sorry."

"Hey, we're alive. They say any landing you can walk away from..."

Jill felt nauseous. When — if — they were rescued, Robbie would find out that she stole a plane and she flew without even being a pilot. She suddenly realized how totally foolish that was. They could have died. She could have killed the only guy she ever really liked.

She had to confess to Robbie even if he hated her after. She had to tell him she's not really a pilot, just a stupid thief who can't even remember to fill up the gas tanks.

She looked at his blood-soaked shirt and said, "Robbie, there's something I have to tell you."

"Look!" Robbie pointed to a nearby dirt road. A park ranger SUV was tearing down it, kicking up a whirlwind of dust. "Someone saw us crash."

The ranger pulled up to them and squealed to a stop.

"Are you two okay?" He grabbed a first aid kit from the back of his SUV.

Jill shuddered. He was going to find out she stole this plane and wrecked it. She was in some deep doo-doo.

With a sudden roar, the gas puddle ignited and flamed up into an orange and black ball, igniting the wings. Jill instinctively ducked. Her jerky movement set her ankle off into a riot of excruciating pain. From twenty feet away, she could feel the heat on her face from the inferno.

The ranger helped her into his SUV and Robbie joined her in the back.

As they drove away, Jill felt tears sting her cheek. What was she thinking? How could she have been so irresponsible?

After the ranger called the fire department, he asked, "Which one of you was the pilot?" He was a large man with the seriousness of his law enforcement job filling him up with a look of importance. She trembled.

"Me," Jill's voice broke.

"What's your name?"

"Jillian Townsend." Again her voice failed her. She tried clearing her throat.

"You look awfully young to be a pilot. Do you have your license?"

"Working on it" was what she should have said, but instead she said, "You can get a license at seventeen."

"I know that, but I also know student pilots can't take passengers for flights until they have their license and he doesn't look like your flight instructor." The ranger motioned to Robbie.

"My dad died," Jill blurted out. It was the only thing she could think of. The Dead Dad Excuse worked for a lot of things. It got her out of any class she wanted, sending her off to the counselors' office — of course that was only when she couldn't stop the darn tears from falling out her eyes at the most embarrassing times. But would the DD Excuse save her from Mr. Frib when he found out he no longer had an airplane?

She was toast. Not to mention what Mom would do to her. Hell hath no fury like a Mom disobeyed. Her stomach flopped and she thought she might puke again. She cracked the window open and tried to breathe through the pain knifing up her leg.

"You okay?" Robbie asked. He was still holding her sleeve to his head.

"I hope it doesn't leave a scar."

"I don't." He lowered his voice. "How else will I break into the story of the time this chick took me flying and we crashed in the desert?"

She wanted to kiss him for his efforts to try to make her feel better, but she didn't want to feel better. She needed to be punished for getting him hurt. Whatever Mom dished out, she'd take it. Oh God, what if the cops send her to jail? Wasn't this grand theft or something? Was that a felony? Would she still be considered a juvenile? Sometimes when you really piss off the powers that be, they upgrade you to an adult and throw you in jail with the murderers and crack dealers. *Course, that would be too good for me.* Jill stuck her head out the window and tried to breathe into her tight lungs.

They pulled up to the place she hated. The place she had never wanted to go to ever again.

31 Load Factor

The hospital reeked of bleach and barf. It was the last place on earth Jill ever wanted to end up.

"I have to tell you something." She eased back on the hospital bed.

Robbie stepped closer. It had only taken the four hours they had been in the emergency room for Jill to work up the courage for a confession. Robbie had already been sewn up and bandaged but Jill was still waiting to be seen. Her ankle was probably starting to heal crooked. Mom hadn't arrived yet and Robbie was waiting to be picked up by his parents. The hospital was a two-hour drive from Big Bear Lake in some podunk desert-rat town, but it was busy enough to make Jill wait forever to get her ankle set back into place. She hated the smell of hospitals, the harsh lighting, the sounds of screaming. Oh wait, the only one screaming was her, inside her head. A wicked headache throbbed so badly, she wished she could scream out loud.

She hated hospitals and Dad hadn't even needed one. He was dead on arrival. But she had found out in a hospital. In a sterile place with these gray walls and cold florescent lighting. She had thought she was going to see Dad and braced herself for how he would look, but as it turned out, she never saw him again. No goodbyes. Nothing. Jill shivered.

Robbie sat on the edge of her bed waiting for her to continue.

Jill looked at him trying to force words out of her mouth.

"You don't have to say anything," Robbie's voice was soft and comforting. It made her feel worse. "Stuff happens. That's life."

She wanted to tell him she didn't have a pilot's license and had no business flying someone else's plane. That her family didn't have a plane and she had never flown to Montana with Dad. That she was just a dreamer who screwed up. Big time.

"In the car with the ranger," Robbie started, "you brought up that your dad is dead. This must be really hard for you… Crashing and all…

It must remind you…"

Jill squeezed her eyes shut and pinched her thigh. She didn't want to cry but lately the tears came uninvited.

"You don't have to talk about it," he consoled.

She couldn't. If she tried, she would just end up blubbering. She kept her eyes shut tight trying to get the emotional tsunami to subside.

Saved by the doctor finally showing up: a woman in a white coat pulled the curtain back and picked up Jill's chart.

"I'm Doctor Myeum," the doctor scribbled on the chart. "You crashed a plane?"

"There was a gas leak," Robbie said. "It wasn't her fault."

Jill gulped. She had to tell him before he found out in the newspaper or something. She could see the headlines now: STUPID GIRL FLIES PLANE WITHOUT GAS AND CRASHES IN THE DESERT.

"The police are waiting to talk to you," Doctor Myeum said. "So, let's get you fixed up." The doctor poked at Jill's leg but she didn't scream. She bit her lip. Robbie hovered near the back of the curtain.

"Why don't you wait outside?" Doctor Myeum said to him.

When the doc finished torturing Jill's ankle, she hobbled out to the waiting room on crutches. She had a few stitches and bandages on her face and hand, but it didn't hurt too much — only a sharp stabbing pain taking turns with a dull throbbing ache. Robbie was gone, but Mom was there. Her face was purple with anger. She didn't speak. She glared death rays at Jill. Bre and Kelly were in PJs, clinging to teddy bears, instinctively knowing not to touch the mad, mad mommy. Their little hands would probably melt off if they got too close.

The look on Mom's face sent shivers down Jill's sore spine. Fear gripped her chest and squeezed. Okay, maybe jail would be better.

A uniformed police officer approached Jill. "Young lady, I need a few words."

Jill choked on some air.

"Alan Frib in Big Bear Lake says he's missing an airplane. Would you happen to know anything about that?"

Jill looked at Mom. Was it possible for her to combust on the spot? She could swear Mom's feet were smoldering the linoleum beneath her.

"This will go better if you tell the truth, young lady," the police officer said.

"I rented Mr. Frib's plane, but I forgot to fill it up with gas. I'm sorry." She leaned away on her crutches.

"Sorry?" Mom seethed. "You're sorry. Well, okay, then," she said sarcastically.

"Mrs. Townsend," the police officer said, "where's Mr. Townsend?"

Mom's face changed from the storm of the century into broken levies. Tears spilled over. She washed up in the chair behind her.

"He died," Kelly said. Jill doubted Kelly even knew what that meant, even after all this time.

Mom sobbed. "This would have never happened if he were here. We've all been upset..."

Jill let herself cry and then her sisters joined in. The police officer looked frightened of the four crying women out of control and stepped back.

"We can finish this..." he backed up, "later. Go home and I'll speak with you tomorrow." He stood at the door, as far away as possible.

A nurse came from behind the counter and stood agasp at the scene. The police officer addressed her. "I'm releasing this girl to the custody of her mother." He held out a card. "Have the girl report to my office at the station at three tomorrow." She took the card. As he left, the nurse gathered the two youngest in a hug. "Shhh, it's okay."

Yeah, right. Things were about to get worse for Jill and her broken, messed-up family. There is no future for felons.

32 Center of Gravity

Even the crystals in the window didn't shine. Their glass was dark and cloudy. Like the sky outside the window in the Judsudeson kitchen. Like her entire being.

Jill didn't touch the salad Nikka set on the table. Nikka quietly ate hers with hardly any movement, looking up at Jill every once in a while. After she got home from the hospital, Jill had been allowed to go to Nikka's to pick up her homework assignments. Evidently, nothing, not even crashing, could circumvent the institution of a mother's belief in the rightness, the necessity, of homework completion. Although Jill suspected the real reason Mom had dropped her off at Nikka's was Mom's inability to look at Jill without fury coursing through her veins.

Jill shifted her crutches out of the way so she could put her throbbing ankle up on the seat across the table. She didn't care about the pain. It almost felt good to hurt physically, as if it were an outlet for the agony she felt inside her heart.

"You would probably be more comfortable on the sofa," Nikka offered.

She felt too heavy to budge. "I can't move. I'm having a Heavy-Gravity Day." Sometimes Jill thought the Earth traded gravitational pull with Jupiter and rooted her like uranium to one spot. It took great energy to sit up. This was one of those days. Mom seemed to live trapped by gravity nearly every day.

Nikka knew what she meant. She let a tear recycle into her mouth. "I'm scared for you."

"I know. I could go to jail."

"What are you going to do?"

"I don't know." Jill gave in to the sickness in her chest. "I miss my dad." She let tears come, wincing at the pain they unleashed in her ribs. "I miss him so much. I miss the way my family used to be. Having plans. I miss what I thought my life was. I miss what I thought the world was. Suddenly, it changed. No one warned me. No one told me everything was going to change so much I wouldn't even recognize my own life." Jill could barely get the words out through the sobs. Nikka cried too.

Jill continued through the tears. "How could this happen? I don't even know one thing for sure, Nikka. Not one thing. What's real? How could it be this bad? My life is a nightmare."

"You'll be okay," Nikka offered in a voice that tried to sound convinced.

"I wish I could talk to him."

"What would you say?"

Jill thought about it for a second, then replied, "I feel abandoned."

Nikka scooted next to her to hug her. "I'm here." They sat silently for a while.

Tia walked in from her studio room and saw the gloomy faces.

"It can't be that bad," Tia said.

"It is," Nikka said. "Jill's in trouble."

"Again," Jill added.

Tia slid to the cabinets and popped a snack bar in her mouth. "Is it going to be on your permanent record? Because if it isn't, what's the problem? I got in trouble all the time too. You should see what my old alma mater has on me."

"You're an artist."

"I still had to get into college to teach. I wasn't allowed to teach kids, though. You have to be squeaky clean for that. The only squeaky thing on me is my Gellies." Tia stuck her foot out, showing her plastic shoes.

The girls didn't say anything. Jill felt the doom growing larger over her head. If she wasn't all cried out, she would let the tears rip.

"So, what's up?" Tia asked.

Jill didn't say anything or even look up.

"Apologies go a long way. Did you try that?" Tia sounded hopeful. Naive.

"I don't think sorry will cover this," Jill said.

"You'd be surprised what genuine remorse can do. You've been through a lot. You're mom hasn't been there for you and your dad only died a year ago. It's understandable—"

"The Dead Daddy Excuse isn't working anymore. Especially not after this."

"Keep trying. I forgive you." Tia hugged Jill's shoulders. "No matter what you did."

"I stole a plane and took Robbie for a ride, then crashed it."

"Oh." Tia sat down. She didn't say anything for an eternity. Then, finally, "Are they pressing charges?"

"Probably. I have to meet with the police tomorrow." Jill's dread reflected in her tone. "Now I'll never get to fly."

Tia looked away. That was the worst. Why didn't she say something? Anything.

"Tia?"

"Yeah, that's a doozy. I had no idea that's what you were going to say. Sweetie, you might have to just live with the consequences. But at least you're alive. You could have died in the crash. Let's count the blessings we can…"

Oh, no, not Tia! Why wasn't she saying something encouraging? Why wasn't she saying "screw it, you don't need a clean record" or something. Why wasn't she saying "your youth is for making mistakes?" "Live and learn." Compassion and all that. If Tia was looking at her with that "you're screwed" expression, then she really was. There's no hope for her future.

Dad, I really, really blew it.

Then, the thought occurred what he might say, almost as if he did say it in her head, "At least you have a future."

He didn't have a future. As messed up as her life was, at least she had a life. Jill sighed and decided there was nothing she could do but make the best of it. Maybe there was another Robbie out there. Maybe there was another dream…

At this point, it was only important that she try to get through this — whatever happened at the police station tomorrow.

33 Pull Back

"**Y**ou're here?" Jill was surprised to see Claire at her front door. Even though Jill hadn't finished cleaning up breakfast, she invited her in, hobbling on her crutches.

"Well, yeah." Claire put her hands on her hips. "When a student of mine crashes, I'm going to want to know what happened."

Jill felt proud that Claire called her a "student of mine" then immediately ashamed. She had no right to feel proud of anything after what she did.

"What happened?" Claire helped herself to a wooden chair at the dining room table. The girls looked up from the TV. Bre descended on her as fast as a dog jumps up to greet a visitor. She climbed up in Claire's lap. With a smile, Claire helped her settle.

"And who are you?" Claire asked Bre.

"Bre. I'm three."

"No, you're not," Kelly corrected. She came over to stare at the visitor too. "You're four."

"Oh, yeah. I forgot." She amused herself with Claire's watch, a square face on a plain black band. Jill dropped her crutches and collapsed in a chair across from Claire at the table.

"Are you okay?" Claire asked Jill.

"Fractured ankle. Broken ribs. Mostly."

"You were so lucky. You know that, don't you? It's unusual for someone to survive a crash like that, where you were, in rough terrain, without knowing how to land."

Jill didn't feel very lucky.

"What happened?" Claire asked.

"I wanted to rent Mr. Frib's plane and—"

"You're not allowed to solo yet. I haven't signed you off for that."

"I know."

"Well, why'd you do it?"

"I don't know," Jill stammered.

"You're going to have to do better than that," Claire said.

She didn't wait long before continuing, "You not only took your life and your passenger's life in your hands but things like this are bad for everyone. Every crash hurts aviation. Not to mention the heat I'm getting. I showed you how to take off, how to fly, and you didn't even have permission from your parents. And now this. How could you be so irresponsible?" Bre climbed down from Claire's lap and ran to the TV. Kelly stepped back until she reached the curtains and slowly tangled herself up in them. "How could you do this?"

"I don't know." Tears welled up in Jill's eyes.

Claire seemed like she was trying to swallow her anger. She looked expectantly at Jill. Knowing she had to try to explain, Jill shifted to put her throbbing ankle up on a chair as she made an attempt to answer.

"I … I just wanted to fly so bad. I didn't know if I'd ever get to. You were mad at me. My mom was mad at me. I didn't have the money… I just wanted to fly, but it's so hopeless. Haven't you ever had a dream? I didn't think my dream was ever going to come true."

Claire leaned back in her chair. Her voice was softer. "You have to have training first before you fly alone. You have to learn all the maneuvers for a reason. The protocols are there because they've been tested through time from many who have gone before you. The training exists to help you, to keep you alive." Claire paused. "The procedures are important for you to become a safe pilot. It's very, very serious what you've done."

"I'm so sorry. I just wanted my dream and now I'll never have it. For the rest of my life!" She forced herself to hold away the waterworks. To her surprise, Claire was the one who had tears in her eyes.

"I understand." Claire blinked away her tears quickly. "It's not so different from the situation I got myself into. You remind me of myself. I was a lot like you. Impatient. So impatient I've been blacklisted for the rest of my life."

Jill waited for more, hoping to find out what went wrong in Claire's life.

"You're in too much of a hurry." Claire leaned across the table and spoke so earnestly. Jill had never seen her so open. "Impatience is a lack of faith in yourself."

Claire paused to blink back tears again. "You have to trust yourself. Trust you'll find a way to make your dreams come true. Trust the process." Her voice cracked. She cleared her throat. "If you could find a way to truly believe in yourself, you wouldn't be so impatient that you make bad..." Claire stopped herself. "Do you get what I'm saying? You've been reckless because you don't believe...You've got to believe in yourself and know that what you want will come."

"It's too late. I have to talk to the police today," Jill sighed.

"Stealing from an airport is a felony. There's nothing I can do to help you. No airline will ever hire you now. I'm not sure you'll ever be able to get work as a pilot."

"I know, but—" Jill sank down in her seat. Rivers of sad flash-flooded her heart. She knew it was too late. She had ruined everything.

Claire discreetly wiped her eyes and sat up. "But here's what I think: less than, maybe, one percent would have survived that crash. There must be a reason you did. And living through that makes you the luckiest girl I know. It's more important now than ever before that you learn to trust yourself."

"No matter what happens this afternoon?"

"No matter what. Period." Claire stood. "If I had known that when I was younger, I'd be flying the world in a jet."

"What happened?" Jill asked softly.

"I was impatient."

"I know, but what happened?"

Claire dropped back into her seat. "I'm going to tell you something, but I don't want you to repeat it."

Jill nodded. She had never seen Claire humbled before, even being knocked out by her own plane or getting lost in the fog wasn't as big as whatever Claire was hiding. The woman who was usually as strong as a headwind looked as meek as a breeze now, not even strong enough to make a windsock stand up and point a direction.

"I took a short-cut," Claire's voice broke. She cleared it and continued. "I was in a hurry to get my career going. I didn't know how I was going to pay for all the flight hours I would need to get a job with all the hours of experience they require. So I lied. I falsified my flight records. I said I had more flight hours than I did so I could get hired. I didn't think anyone would find out, but they did."

Claire pressed her palm into her forehead and then smoothed back her bangs. "The airline fired me immediately. After I already had my dream job, I lost it. I lost everything I had worked for because of a few hours. Talk about impatience."

"That's it? You lied about flight time and they fired you? You can never get another airline job your whole life because of that?"

"Lying is serious, Jill. It's not only a lack of integrity and honor, it's a lack of being real. Being authentic. Honoring yourself, not just others." She stood up again. "Well, anyway, you're going to do what you're going to do. I'm just trying to help."

Jill nodded, swallowing back tears.

Claire let herself out.

Jill felt so sad. This was about how bad she felt when Dad died. She couldn't breathe. She had to get fresh air.

Hopping outside to the bright patio, Jill squinted in the sun. She fell onto the deck lounger, put a towel over her head and lay in the bright rays, choking back the agony she felt throughout her mind and body. Where was she navigating her life? She seemed to have gotten so off course, or maybe what she had been attempting to do was just too hard. Sometimes big dreams cause big washouts. Too bad Claire's advice was too late. Maybe the sun could bake all the regret and sadness out of her. The sorrow felt like an elephant taking up residence on her chest. She couldn't breathe in all the way. Her ribs hurt when she tried. *I've ruined my life!*

As much as she wished she could hit rewind, there wasn't anything she wouldn't do to make this week not have happened. Just like the time Dad died.

At that thought, Jill sat up. She refused to lie down and wish for the past to be different. She had to deal. She bolted inside and found Mom sitting in her bed.

"Mom, I don't want you to feel bad but it's been really, really hard. With you zoned out... And now that I've ruined my future, it's really, really bad."

Mom reached for her pills.

"Could you just listen?! Please?"

Mom set the bottle down unopened.

"I don't know if you've ever had a dream that you wanted so much you didn't think right. Have you ever wanted something really,

really bad?"

"I wanted a family," she sniffed.

"If you haven't noticed, we're still here." Jill subtly moved the bottle of pills into the drawer and shut it quietly. "I need you to drive me to Mr. Frib. I have to talk to him before I talk to the police. Okay? I have something I need to say to him right away. It can't wait."

34 Breaks in Overcast

Mom pulled up next to Mr. Frib's hangar. Jill hesitated with her hand on the car door, afraid to get out. "I'm so scared. I don't know what he'll do to me."

"I'll come with you," Mom said.

"Thanks."

Inside his airplane-less hangar, Mr. Frib was putting tools and airplane accessories in boxes, cleaning out his hangar. The shoulders of his bomber jacket hunched over. A stab of guilt ricocheted from her ribs to her foot. On her crutches, she hobbled toward him slowly.

Mr. Frib looked up. "I'm packing up. No sense paying for a hangar when I haven't got an airplane anymore." He sounded upset.

"I'm so sorry," Jill said, wishing she could make it up to him.

"Last night, I thought the plane was stolen," he said gravely. "I didn't know you were going to take it. When I said you could rent my plane, I didn't mean right way, without… some things first. Paperwork. And now this morning they tell me you're not a pilot. A student. I'm not sure I would have rented to a student pilot."

"That's what I was afraid of. I made a huge mistake, Mr. Frib. I'm so sorry. I want to fly so bad and it kind of fried holes in my brain. I didn't think anyone was going to let me. I couldn't stand it. But I know what I did was so wrong and I'm prepared to accept the consequences. But first, I wanted to apologize to you. I owe you at least that."

"And the boy? Why'd you take someone with you?"

"He kind of fries my brain too. I thought I could impress him…" Jill turned red.

Mom stepped forward. "Mr. Frib, I'm Jill's mother and I want to say sorry too. I've been sick to death about my husband's passing and I haven't been there for Jill. I thought she was doing okay. Now I know I was wrong. I blame myself." Mom didn't cry. Jill was proud of her but wished she wouldn't blame herself.

"I thank you both for having the courage to face me. It makes the bitter pill a bit easier to swallow — to know why. I was wondering all last night who could have done this to me and why. Why me? I see now that it hasn't anything to do with me. Helps a little."

He looked at her sternly. "I miss my plane, but I do appreciate you coming here."

He turned, closed up a box and carried it to his car.

Jill looked at Mom and sighed. It felt good to have done that. A little bit of guilt moved off her chest. Mom put her arms around her, the first time since Dad's death.

"Jillian, I'll always love you. You know that, don't you?"

Before she could answer, Mr. Frib came back over. "Listen," he said. "I got a thought. I could use some help with my business and it seems prudent to me to make the best of things, especially" he said under his breath, "since I'm having to explain why my security was so lax." He straightened his back and looked two inches taller. "How about you work for me in exchange for me giving you a second chance?"

"What do you mean?" Jill asked.

"I won't press charges. I'll let the authorities know that you and I had discussed renting out the plane and we had a misunderstanding. Putting this in the light of a misunderstanding is very generous of me. It is an interpretation I'm willing to take. The benefit of the doubt. We did discuss it. I could see how things might have gotten a little mixed up. Do you understand I'm giving you a second chance? Second chances are very rare and you are very lucky, Young Lady."

"Yes! I would be so grateful for a second chance. You have no idea!" Falling over herself, she grabbed his arm and squeezed.

"You'll still have to deal with the FAA because you broke the rule of taking a passenger before you are certificated."

"Yes, yes, I know. When do I report for work?"

"You haven't even asked what it is."

"I'll do anything. Anything. I mean, anything legal and safe and smart and …" She thought her face was going to fall off from smiling. Joy rushed through her. Another chance to start over with her life! She *was* lucky. Everything inside her was jumping up and down. Happy joy shivered in her cheeks and sizzled down her spine. Jill actually wanted to dance. Never in her life had she wanted to dance more. Even her foot felt better.

Mr. Frib handed a card to Mom. "She can start tomorrow after school. Here's the address. You're welcome to come and check it out."

Mom nodded and bowed her head, looking too overwhelmed with gratitude to speak.

Now all Jill had to get through was the police report and the FAA investigation. *Cripes.*

35 Hold Your Heading

"**H**ow'd it go?" Nikka asked. "Am I going to have to visit you in prison? Because, you know, I hate that place," she said facetiously. "You wouldn't believe the nasty chemicals they use to scrub the floors." Today her beige hemp dress was dragging on the ground as she introduced a sun salutation to her yoga routine.

Sitting on the school benches near the basketball court, Jill gazed up at the sky as she waited for a ride home from Mom. The heavens were hazy with smoke from a far-off forest fire, but she still wished she were up there. If she never got to go back in it, at least she could look at it any time she wanted. "Yeah, that's the worst part of prison: chemicals."

"The best part is they feed you for free. Three hots a day!" Nikka teased. "My mom says that's her retirement plan if I don't take her in during her old age. She's gonna commit a crime so she can go to The Big House nursing home."

Jill laughed. "Only Tia."

"So?" Nikka raised her arms in front of Jill, in the Standing Tree pose. "Are you gonna be a jail bird?"

"Nope, probation for two years. But if I screw up during probation, I go to jail."

Nikka looked a little nervous. "And?"

"And the FAA suspended my student license for thirty days and fined me two thousand dollars."

"Whoa, two thousand dollars!"

"Yeah, it doesn't really matter how long I've been suspended from flying because between working off my debt to Mr. Frib and the fine, I'll never be able to afford it anyway."

"You don't seem as upset about that as I thought you'd be. I thought you'd implode on the spot if you couldn't fly."

"Oh, I'm gonna fly. Some day."

Nikka twisted her arms around each other and squatted into the Eagle pose. "Have you seen Robbie yet?"

Everything stopped at the mention of Robbie's name. Jill stopped breathing, her heart stopped beating and the world stopped turning. "No," she expelled in a long exhale.

She pushed him out of her mind and squinted at the bright haze. It would be a good day for flying. The winds were calm and the sun was shining, but it wasn't too hot. The sky wouldn't be mottled very high, only a couple thousand feet. In spite of the smoke, she could smell a whiff of sage and lavender in the air that almost made her feel better. She was doing her best to hold it together, but she felt a gloom move into her chest like a raincloud. Turbulence and all. She had to face the fact that she'd have to give up her dream. It had brought her so much trouble. She couldn't lie to herself anymore. And Robbie was another storm thundering inside her: she had to tell him the truth.

Nikka read her mind. "Do you think he knows? Maybe he's not mad cuz he got to go for a flight. Maybe he's glad he didn't know you were flying illegally so he could get a ride."

Jill felt her shoulders lift a little. She sat up straighter. She needed to change the subject. "Are you really going to the prom? I thought you'd boycott it. Aren't they using Styrofoam or something?"

"It's a dance." Nikka slowed into a deep stretch to the side. Her upper half was sideways. "I can't miss a dance I don't have to drive an hour for. I'm sure the tunes will be lame but at least Cesar and I can get our groove on."

"Wish I was gonna be there to see it."

"Ask Robbie. Cesar says Trevor says Robbie hasn't asked anyone yet. He can't say no to a pilot, even one who crashes. You're the girl who took him beyond the clouds." Nikka winked.

Jill let herself believe it. She liked the idea of going to prom with Robbie, his last big dance in highschool. "That would rock." Jill lost herself in a daydream of being locked in Robbie's arms on the dancefloor. She could nearly feel his face gently against hers.

"There he is now." Nikka pointed with her shoulder. "Go get 'im, Tiger."

Jill laughed and decided to launch, trawling herself over to him.

"Hey." Jill blocked Robbie's path on the walkway to the main buildings.

The stitches on his forehead had scabs around them. She winced.

"Hey." Robbie looked away. Pause, pause, pause. He didn't say anything.

Jill didn't know what to say other than what was on her mind. "Do you have a date for prom?"

"Prom?"

"Yeah, cuz I was wondering if you—"

"You think I can go to prom? After what happened?" Robbie's face was angry. She had never seen him like that before. "You're not a pilot. You haven't even soloed. You lied."

"I have soloed," she blurted out. "I mean, I've flown a plane by myself before. When my instructor was unconscious."

"Whatever. That's not official. You haven't been signed off to solo. You haven't taken the test. You can't just go around lying, thinking the rules don't apply to you. Do you know how much trouble I'm in? They don't believe me that I didn't know. They think I was out joy-riding. That I'm lying. You don't know what you've done. You don't know… They won't let me in now—" He turned away to control his anger.

She didn't know what he was talking about but she had to do something. "I…" She touched his arm, but he stepped back. "I'll tell them you didn't know. I'm so sorry, Robbie. You just wanted to fly so bad, I—"

He rounded on her. "No. No, I didn't want to fly so bad that I'd trash my college acceptance!" He fumed off.

"I'll tell them you didn't know," Jill called after him.

He turned and yelled so that the whole school could hear, "Don't bother. Just leave me alone."

Before Nikka could shelter Jill off-campus, she was crying uncontrollably. With her arm around Jill's waist and carrying her crutches, Nikka guided her to her car and helped her in.

36 Updraft

"**A**re you ready?" Nikka asked.

Jill finished wrapping her ankle in an ace bandage. She had shed her crutches a few days ago and could walk almost like normal. It had been weeks since the Robbie incident and she had managed to get over the humiliation. The heartbreak was a different matter. She hurt that she'd blown it with him but she hurt more that she had spoiled his acceptance to whatever college he was gunning for. And when prom came up as a subject of discussion at school, she shuttered. She bolted away embarrassed from any conversation about what to wear to prom. How could she have been so delusional as to try to ask Robbie to prom?

"Almost ready," Jill said. Bre ran to her with a brush at the dining room table. Jill brushed her hair into two pigtails and called after Kelly. "Are you ready, Kell?"

The only answer she received was some squeak from the bathroom. Both girls were excited about their outing today. Bre's bouncing made it hard to capture all her hair into the ties, but Jill didn't strive for perfection. The girls needed to get out on a snow day. They needed to run. Jill could understand. She needed this too.

"Did you tell your mom what you decided?" Nikka asked quietly. Mom was in her bedroom but Nikka obviously didn't want to take any chances she'd hear.

"Not yet," Jill admitted. "I'm still trying to figure out how to tell her."

"Do you have to tell her?" Nikka turned the music up a little louder and let the beat move her.

"I guess not." Jill finished Bre's hair and sent her to grab her jacket. "But I want to be honest. She should know. What I mean is, I want her to know."

"I'm proud of you. Going for your dream, no matter what you've been through. Making a new plan."

"You realize I can never work for the airlines now, right? I screwed that up forever."

"Really?" Nikka asked with wide eyes. "Forever and ever?"

"I can't believe people think they want someone trustworthy to fly them around," Jill said sarcastically.

"And you still want to be a pilot?" Nikka asked incredulously.

"The sky may not be as open now, but I still want to be up there any way that I can get up."

"I'm glad you're not giving up."

"Not giving up when I make a complete fool of myself, you mean."

"Yeah, whatever. At least you're going for it." Nikka stopped moving. "Even when it's too hard."

Jill noticed Nikka's face cloud over. "You're going for your dream too. You'll probably be a famous artist before I get my wings."

"That's the thing. Being an artist isn't my dream — unless you count my body as the canvas and my beat as the paint."

"You want to be a dancer?"

"Shhh. I can't even say it." Nikka pressed her index finger to her lips.

"Why not?"

Nikka blushed a little. "What if I suck? What if I go out there and everyone's like, 'who does she think she is? Nut-uh. She can't dance.'"

"You're totally the dance goddess of all time."

"What if I can't cut it?"

"At least you'll have fun trying, right? If you're having fun and you love it, who cares?"

"You miss flying?" Nikka looked at her knowingly.

"Soooo much." Jill gripped her chest. "I can't remember what the sky looked like. I'm dying for a flight."

Nikka shot her a look.

Jill smirked and picked up a stack of mail from the table. "Don't worry. I'm gonna learn the mere mortal way to fly. Get me some training." Jill opened an envelope in the pile. "Oh my god, Nikka! Nikka! Nikka! Nikka!"

"What? What? What?"

"I got it!" Jill realized she needed to lower her voice. She looked toward the hallway and then whispered. "I got it!"

"Got what?"

"It was so long ago that I applied, I forgot about it."

"Got what?"

"A scholarship," Jill nearly yelled.

"What?"

"I applied for a scholarship for flight training from Women in Aviation International and I got it."

"No way!" Nikka squealed.

Jill gently put a hand over Nikka's mouth. "This means I can start lessons again when the suspension's over. I don't need to find the money to pay for my license!"

This time Jill put her hand over her own mouth. She was having trouble keeping her voice down. "I'm going to be a pilot!"

"But don't you have to pay the fine first?"

"Yeah, so, what's your point?"

Nikka laughed. "Only you."

"You still think there's a family curse?" Jill demanded.

"I don't know. Major stuff has happened to you — both good and bad."

"This is so very, very good. I had to write an essay. This means they liked it. This means there are other pilots who want to help me become a pilot too. This is so awesome."

"They just give you the money to take lessons?"

"Yes, as long as you promise to try to pay it forward in the future. The idea is to help someone someday the way they are helping you. That's their only requirement."

"Cool." Nikka wrapped Bre in a scarf and beanie. "I like these people. They got anything for dancers?"

"Only if you want to do your dancing in the sky." Jill dashed for the door. "Let's jet. I'm feeling a million times better. You have no idea."

"You think your mom will let you use the scholarship?"

Jill's happy crashed. She ran out of the house before she could think about what Nikka said.

Barreling up the hill in the forest behind Jill's house, Nikka held two trash can lids. Jill's hands were free to help Bre out of the snow every time she fell before Kelly stomped on her. The snow had decided to fall all at once, three feet in one day. They huffed and trudged toward the top. Since the schizophrenic weather had delivered a snowstorm in May, it would quickly melt away with the bright sun beating on the mountain today.

"What's Cesar wearing to prom?" Jill asked. "He doesn't seem like the type to suit up. He has to put on the bling, you know, a stupid tux. And you'll have to wear an evening gown."

"He's got something retro to wear but don't expect to see me in some J-Lo-wanna-be, shrink-wrapped dress."

"Yeah, right. Like you could even find organic hemp with sequins. Even in the snow, you'd rather wear soaking cotton than waterproof plasticized snowpants. Is polyester supposed to be bad for the planet or something?" Jill feigned as she held out the sides of her snowpants.

"Not everyone chooses comfort over conscience. You'll be sorry when there's no more real estate without stinking landfills."

"Sorry, but dry." A smile spread across Jill's face.

Nikka laughed at her. "You are too happy."

"Scholarship, baby." Jill high-fived Bre.

"Your mom has to let you fly now," Nikka said as she set the trash can lids in the snow to zip up Kelly's jacket against the biting wind. "That's such a good omen. A gift from the heavens."

"I know, right?" Jill panted from the steep climb.

Nikka helped Kelly over a fallen tree and they resumed trudging up the hill. They reached the top and sat on the lids. Kelly teamed with Jill and they set off sledding down the hill. Bre squealed and clutched Nikka.

As Jill and Kelly picked up speed toward the bottom, Kelly's foot dug into the snow and sent them straight for a tree stump. They hit it hard and flew off the lid.

Nikka and Bre rushed to the crash site. "You alright?"

Jill knocked the snow out of her hair and picked Kelly up. "We're fine." Kelly's face contorted into a cry that sounded put on.

Nikka tried to push the lid back into shape. "Must be that ugly Townsend curse. Face it: you guys are disaster-bent. Always a crash waiting to happen."

Nikka meant it as a joke, but Jill felt the breath go out of her. She didn't sleep well last night thinking about all that had happened to her. She had never wanted an ordinary life, but she didn't think she could stand many more surprises. Now that she had money to fly, she could get back in the sky. The thought thrilled her and terrified her at the same time.

She grabbed the dented lid from Nikka and ran back up the hill. Kelly's pseudo-tears turned to laughter as she followed her for more head-banging fun.

37 Indicated Airspeed

Sitting at lunch on the tables beyond the school courtyard, Nikka seemed calmer than Jill had seen her since forever. Only her shoulder kept the beat of Cesar's portable speakers. Cesar shrugged off the quinoa and couscous Nikka offered him and sat so close to her, she could hardly move the fork to her own mouth. Jill munched leftovers from food Mom had made. Well, okay, a frozen dinner Mom had nuked, but still.

Jill tried not to watch them, but it was hard to miss. Nikka acted all cool, but Jill could tell she really liked him. She saw Nikka relax into his arm when he slipped it around her waist. They kissed, oblivious to her, or so she thought.

When Cesar pulled out of the kiss, he looked around and caught Jill peeking.

"We're getting a limo," Cesar said. "For prom. You should reserve a spot."

"She has to get a date first," Nikka offered. She didn't mean it in a bad way but there's hardly a way you can say something like that in a good way.

Jill flushed with embarrassment. "Don't make fun of the love-challenged. The only way I'm ever going to a dance is if the walls are padded and I can wear a helmet."

Nikka turned to Cesar to explain, "There's a curse on her family. That's why stuff happens — she crashed a plane and lost her one chance to have a boyfriend this year."

"That doesn't sound like a curse," Cesar said.

"There were other things," Nikka said softly. Jill was grateful she didn't explain about her first "instructor" dying during her first flying lesson. Once Vern's autopsy revealed he died of natural causes, the manhunt was off, and Jill never wanted it mentioned again.

Nikka also didn't bring up the biggest bad break that had happened to Jill's family.

"I believe in a jinx," Cesar said, "but that's more like a strange coincidence. Something really weird happening, that's bad, but really unusual."

Jill and Nikka shared a look.

"Yeah," Jill said. "There were things like that, too."

Cesar saw the girls exchanging a look and shrugged it off. "You need a charm to break it," Cesar said. "My mom doesn't go anywhere without her Saint Christopher medallion. She believes it protects her."

"Yeah," Nikka said, her eyes lighting up, "you just need a guardian angel, that's all."

Cesar pulled Nikka closer into his chest. "Some people believe that when someone in your family dies, they become that."

Nikka plunged forward with the idea igniting her eyes. "You need a charm to break the curse. Something like what his mom has—"

"So," Jill interrupted, "what you're saying is Cesar's mom will live forever because she has a Saint Christopher necklace?" Her voice dripped with sarcasm, "Hmm, yeah, that explains why all those people who carry charms never die or get injured."

"It couldn't hurt," Nikka sounded frustrated. "If you're going to start flying again, you need all the help you can get."

Jill just smiled and took a bite of her twice-nuked lasagna. She didn't know if she believed in the Townsend curse, or charms, or fate, or anything else for that matter. She didn't really care. She could accept almost anything as long as she got to fly again.

"Whatever will be, will be, right?" Jill turned to end the conversation. She looked around at her classmates grouped around tables. She heard Nikka and Cesar kissing and turned away some more.

Crossing the courtyard, Robbie glanced over at Jill. Jill lowered her eyes. She could hear that Trevor stopped Robbie to talk to him. She couldn't make out what they were saying but suddenly lost her appetite and rose. She hadn't talked to Robbie since he yelled at her.

It wasn't that easy avoiding him at a small school, but he helped. When she walked through the school halls passing him, he looked right through her, like he had done before the crash. As an actor, he was excellent. It almost seemed he didn't know she was alive. But she knew he saw her. She could feel him loathing her from the corner of his eyes. It made her feel small and terrible. She stood and gathered her things.

Nikka parted from Cesar long enough to ask, "Where you going?"

"I'm going to history early because that's what kind of geek I am."

"You say that like it's a bad thing," Cesar joked.

Jill specifically took the south path, away from Robbie. She heard quick footsteps and felt a hand on her shoulder.

"Jill." It was Robbie's voice. Jill's knees went weak. Her body betrayed her. She felt a thrill at his hand on her shoulder. She loved hearing his voice, but she was scared to face him.

As much as she didn't want to, she turned and looked at him.

"Hey," he said.

"Hey," she managed to squeak out.

"Thank you."

"Thank you?" For hurting you? For crashing? For putting you in harm's way? For being a complete idiot?

"Yes, for telling everyone I didn't know about your schemes. I'm not in trouble except for being stupid enough to believe you. No one's sore at me anymore. I've been returned to active status in CAP and the AFA recruiter has put me back on the list. All punishments lifted. How's it going for you? No jail time, huh?"

"Probation. As long as I don't do anything else wrong for two years, I'll be 'expunged'." Jill made quotation marks with her fingers.

"That's good."

"The FAA fined me two thousand dollars and suspended my student license."

"Ouch."

"I deserve that and more. I'm so sorry, Robbie."

"I know."

"Can you ever forgive me?" She held her breath. He didn't answer for a long moment.

"Maybe. Under two conditions..."

Ut-oh. This wasn't sounding good. Would she have to pay another fine or work off another debt? She'd be forty before she got out from under this.

"Number one: when you're a licensed pilot, you know, certificate and all — and, by the way, I'll be checking the original copy — you can take me for a real trip."

"Done." She felt a wave of relief flood her.

"And number two: go to prom with me."

"What?" This was unreal. What changed? How could he want the felon FlyGirl to be his date for prom?

Since she didn't answer, he explained, "I thought it would be the best way to end the year I had my first crash — I mean — flight, in the co-pilot's seat, with a brief, brief moment at the controls. It seems appropriate to top off a year like that with the culprit." Grinning, he crossed his arms over his chest.

"Oh." She felt disappointed and happy at the same time. It was awesome that Robbie was not only talking to her again but that he asked her out. But she was disappointed he was asking her because they had a history or something. Some survivor thing, or maybe he had a great story to tell his friends. Going to the prom with the plane thief. She was just a devious "culprit" who had taken him on a flight he'd never forget.

"I was really, really mad you lied to me," Robbie said. "And come on, of all the dumbass things — but I can say one thing for you, girl." He smiled. "You've got guts. I just hope you don't land in jail."

"My cowboy days are over. I'm minding my Alpha, Bravo, Charlies now. Did I mention how sorry I am?"

He smiled at her. She felt herself melt as she looked at his lips. She wished so much he would kiss her. She told herself she was being greedy. It was enough that he had forgiven her and that they would go to his prom together. A culprit trophy on his arm. She giggled at herself, releasing too much giddiness, and reeled herself back in.

"You didn't answer." Robbie said.

Jill's mind was a haze. "Answer?"

"Prom?"

"Oh. Yes. When is it?" Jill asked even though she knew the answer. Well, she knew the date before her mind went blank with overwhelming jubilation.

"June 17th. Saturday, next week." A week and a half away.

The cloudiness in her head was still swirling, confusing her. She tried to think of something to say, to pull herself out of the torrent of happiness, to continue the conversation like a normal person. "Cesar said there's still room in the limo they're taking." She immediately wished she could pull the words back and stuff them in her mouth. What a stupid thing to say! To suggest he pay for a limo. He must think it awfully forward.

"We're not going in a limo," Robbie said. "I have something

else in mind."

"Yeah?"

"It's a surprise." Her face contorted into a frown. She hated surprises — even from Robbie. She had had enough in her life.

"Don't worry. It has nothing to do with Trevor's Death Defyers project."

Before she could ask what that was, the bell rang. Jill jumped. She had forgotten all about school. Did such a thing really exist? Something so ordinary as fifth period was breaking the spell. Robbie started to walk toward the classrooms, motioning for Jill to walk with him. She forced her legs to obey, but they felt as weak and trembly as after she got out of a plane. He didn't seem to notice her stilted cadence. When they reached her class, Jill paused at the door and risked another look into his eyes.

"I'll call you." He said and left for his class.

Jill blocked the doorway, staring after him, until her classmates nearly mowed her down trying to maneuver around her.

When? All her mind could think was when would he call her?

38 Restricted Airspace

When Robbie had said he'd call her, Jill thought he had meant after school. But he didn't call after school. In fact, it had been five days she listened acutely for the phone to ring and still he had not called. As she studied in her room, Jill was beginning to believe something had gone wrong. It was a dream she had imagined, or Robbie had changed his mind. Maybe he found out about a lie she had not yet confessed to. Surely there were more lies she couldn't remember. That's what made the truth so convenient: you didn't have to try to remember the stories you've told. Was there something else Robbie had discovered? Since they didn't have classes together, she had to look for him at breaks and after school. She was tempted to sneak out and see if Robbie were at CAP. She wanted to ask him why he hadn't called and why she hadn't seen him at school except at a distance. Was he avoiding her? Would she even know if he changed his mind about prom?

As Jill tried to concentrate on her flight manual, she pushed Robbie out of her mind. She wouldn't let a boy throw her off her game again. She had to be ready for her next lesson even though Mom was still forbidding it. Jill wanted to be ready when the time came.

Pulling the book closer, she fought hard to concentrate. She wouldn't sneak out. If she did leave the house later, after she conquered the theory of aerodynamics, she would do it out the front door. Grounded didn't mean she had to be a complete shut-in.

Her eyes looked up at her doorframe just as Mom appeared in it.

"Whatcha reading?" Mom asked. She was holding something behind her back that Jill couldn't see.

"Flight theory. It's incredible. I still can't figure out what makes an airplane fly."

"Money," Mom said.

"Technically, it's lift. Lift is created from the shape of the wings, the Bernoulli effect. But it's such an amazing concept that I can't wrap my mind around it."

"How 'bout you lift your butt to the kitchen and help with dinner?"

"Let me finish this chapter first."

Hesitating, Mom hovered halfway in the room, halfway in the hall. "I got your note," Mom declared.

"Which one?" Jill asked.

Mom pulled her hand out from behind her back. She held a crumpled pile of pink Post-its.

"I'm going to fly." Jill straightened the pillows behind her back. She knew what was coming and it made her antsy. "I'm going to be a pilot. I just thought it would help you accept that."

Mom leaned against the doorframe. "That's what it says here." She held up the Post-its. "Do you think this is going to work?" Mom crossed to the little blue trash can and dumped them in.

Rage spurt up throughout Jill and she sat bolt upright, tossing her book aside. "You can't stop me. Once I'm eighteen, you can't stop me."

"The scholarship expires within six months."

"I know," Jill seethed. She tried to control her rage but it hurled out her words. "If I don't start it soon, they give it away to someone who's more dedicated. But it doesn't matter. I'll get a full-time job the second I turn eighteen and every dime I make will go toward flying. If it takes me my whole life, I'll still do it."

Mom stepped backwards to lean against the doorframe again. "You're still on that, huh? What about college?"

"I won't be able to afford both college and flight training. As it is, the loans for flight training will take my whole life to pay back. But I'm not changing my mind. Even if you make me miss the opportunity of the scholarship." Jill heard the hardness in her voice, but she couldn't back down. She was determined. Nothing else mattered. It would be a tragedy if Mom made her miss out on the scholarship, but she would get over it. She would find a way. She looked up at Mom and saw her face had gone pale. Something changed between them. Something was lost. She could see that Mom understood something had changed between them.

Mom backed out of the bedroom and left silently.

Jill jumped up and slammed the door. She couldn't help herself. She had so much passion and rage swirling in her, she had to do something to express it. She leaned against the door and tried to get ahold of herself. She felt the barrier of the door. The symbolism didn't escape her. She had just shut Mom out of her life. She shuttered and softened into a sob. She felt like an orphan. Why did Dad have to leave?

Alone in her room, she looked at the book dropped on the floor and vowed that next time she had the chance to get in a plane, she would see it differently. Each lesson had been a gift. Each moment in the air was far more of a gift than she had given it credit for. She should have never messed things up the way she did, because it only made it harder now.

She sighed and picked up her book. "Sometime my day will come," she told herself. "And I'll be ready."

After half an hour of studying, Jill ventured to the kitchen to make dinner. All the anger had released her as she read.

Mom was at her laptop on the dining room table and looked worse than Jill thought possible. She had a new fear in her eyes. She had seen another way a parent can lose their child other than the perils of the world.

"We've gotta talk." Mom lumbered to the kitchen and put water in a pan on the stove. "I really can't stand how afraid I am for you. I worry so much about you up in the air, flying."

"Then, don't." Jill took out vegetables from the fridge and started chopping. "Life is never going to be as safe and guaranteed as you want it. And if there's anything I learned from this, Mom, it's that I want to fly more than ever. I want to be a pilot. You don't have to understand."

"I don't understand."

"That much is obvious, Mom." Jill got down pasta from the cabinet. "But maybe you could trust me a little. I know I don't deserve it, but it's different now."

"I can't take any more loss," Mom said, shaking her head.

"Like I can? You're making me lose my life. Mom, life is for living. Full throttle."

Mom found pasta sauce and opened the jar.

Jill tossed the vegetables in a sauté pan. "Look at it this way: for an accident-prone family, we're getting better. I walked away. Next time, I might even have a real landing, on pavement and everything."

"Not funny, Jillian."

With heavy eyes, Mom took a long look at her, leaned against the counter, then spoke. "Most accidents are pilot error — I looked it up." She tried to smile but it was a sad smile. "If I let you... You promise me, you'll be a good pilot? You promise me, I won't lose you? You promise me, you'll make the right decisions up there?"

"I promise. I'll be the best pilot there is." Jill hugged her. "That's why I'm studying so much. And I'm gonna learn everything I can."

Mom took another long look at her. "You don't have anything to prove." Mom put her arms around Jill. "I love you no matter what you do, and in this case," she chuckled, "in spite of what you do."

"I know. But sometimes when you hold on too tight, you strangle what you love."

Mom pulled away and crinkled her face. "What?"

"If you love someone, set her free." Her determination was a different kind of strength now. After what she had been through, she knew nothing was going to make her back down from what was in her heart. "I have to do this, Mom. Like I've told you, I feel it in my bones. They're part fiberglass."

Mom let go of her. "Okay... okay. I guess I can't break your wings and keep you in the nest forever. ... Can I?"

"No, Fancy Pants, you can't. So stop trying!"

"Okay."

Jill jumped up and down. "I'm really going to fly?" She hopped to the living room and lunged onto the carpet, flipping a summersault when she saw her sisters hovering in the hallway. Her sisters took that as a cue to dog pile her. "You still have two other chances for safe little ballerinas." Jill tickled her sisters and listened to the laughter like it was music.

She sang them a silly song to make them laugh, "Aim high, cuz if you aim low, that's probably where you'll go."

"There's one thing," Mom said as Kelly ran to her and latched to her side, standing on her foot with arms locked around her waist, "you have to pay for it all yourself. All your flight training. All your college. Whatever you decide to do. Your family needs whatever money we have now. There's no college fund. And anything you find to sell, we need it. Understand me?"

Jill grabbed Bre's foot. "We oughtta be able to get good money for this foot." She tickled it. Bre screamed laughter. "What else can we sell? How about this elbow?"

"No!" Bre screamed and climbed up Jill's back.

"Go away, then. You're no good to me." Jill piggybacked her into the kitchen to turn off the burners. Mom followed with Kelly still attached to her. Jill set Bre in front of Kelly. "You," Jill said to Kelly, "Captain Caveman, I bring you offering. Bony but tasty." She nibbled on Bre's ankle, erupting more screaming laughter. Kelly tried to chew on Bre's hand, but she was flailing around too fast.

"Let's play hide and seek," Jill said. "You hide. I'll seek." The girls darted away into their usual hiding places. Kelly covered herself with the curtains, her feet showing beneath, and Bre crouched behind the chair next to the TV. Jill counted loudly as she walked down the hall and into her room.

She closed her door and sat at her computer. She had a few minutes before her sisters would come looking for her. Time to drool. On the Web, she found the page she read, as she had done many times before: AVIATION GROUND SCHOOL — WE GUARANTEE YOU'LL BE READY TO SOLO. She'd love to go to that ground school in Houston, but how was she supposed to pay for it? The ground portion taught all things she needed to know for the written test and the oral exam that the FAA examiner would give her. The scholarship covered flight lessons only.

Just then, thrill bumps shot down her arms. She had a scholarship! She ripped a piece of paper from her notebook. She had to find Claire right after she got Mom to sign permission for training.

39 Advise When On Top

"**I** have it!" Jill rushed in the hangar and pronounced. Only Jack was there, working on some fiberglass molding. Jill deflated. It was the first time all week Claire's hangar was open and she wasn't even here.

"Have what?" Jack looked up from the sticky, smelly gunk he was applying to the connection between the wing and the fuselage of Claire's new plane. It was looking more and more like a plane every day. The cowling was off the engine, but the wings and tail were attached.

"My mom's going to let me fly and I won a scholarship. I'm doing it! I'm gonna get back up."

"That's great. Really no sense trying to cage a bird."

"What's that?" Jill pointed to the smelly stuff in Jack's hands.

"Epoxy for the molding." He splayed more on.

"I want to get my lessons going as soon as possible. Do you think Claire will teach me? I kinda blew it."

"Everyone makes mistakes. Some mistakes even turn out good." Jack stretched across the wing to reach the other end and glopped on more goop.

"Yeah, but this was a doozy. I totally blew it."

"I seem to remember a mistake or two she made." He didn't sound too concerned. Jill knew he liked having her near home, instead of stationed at some airport halfway across the country.

"Can you talk to her for me? I think she's avoiding me. She hasn't returned my texts."

"Well, hon, she's got some trouble. The powers that be won't approve her expansion. Seems we built the plane for nothing." Jack's face looked worried. "She needs a backup pilot attached to her business before they'll sign off on her plans."

"Aren't there any commercial pilots around here?"

"None she can hire. She has her reasons. I'll let her explain that." Jack mixed up some more epoxy. "If I were a pilot…"

"I know a good teacher. Why don't you learn to fly?"

"Eh," he dismissed it. "Too old."

"Could you ask Claire to talk to me, please?"

"I'll see what I can do." He bit open a plastic bag. "But it wouldn't hurt to wait for your feet to reach the pedals, would it?"

"They reach. Especially in my six-inch platforms," Jill joked. "I need to log hours as soon as possible. For the scholarship. I need to get it started before they give it to someone else. Will you tell her?"

Jack nodded. "For you, doll, anything." He grinned warmly.

40 Rate of Climb

Jill had missed Claire again. She looked around the hangar, but it was locked. She walked back toward the flightline and lobby. A quiet Monday afternoon, nothing was happening on the airfield. A plane in the distance roared to life and taxied away. Too bad. In an epiphany, Jill had realized a great solution was presenting itself. If only she could tell Claire about it.

Then, the door from the lobby swung open. Out walked Claire with her gear.

"Look who's here: Jivin' Jill," Claire said. "What do you have up your sleeve today?"

"Can you give me lessons again?"

"I heard your mom gave in." Claire could walk brisker than anyone. Jill had to nearly run to keep up. "Jack told me. You've won him over."

"It's just that I have this opportunity now. The scholarship. I can't waste it."

When Claire reached her plane, the 150, she threw her bag inside. At a spigot, Claire dumped soap in a bucket and poured water in. Jill picked up a sponge. "I wash Mr. Frib's new plane every week. I could wash yours, too."

"You'll have to do better than that." Claire carried the bucket over to her plane and started scrubbing it with the soapy water.

Jill stood directly in front of her. "I'm so sorry. Please forgive me. Please teach me."

Claire turned away, scrubbing the elevators.

"Listen," Jill said, "I'm turning seventeen in January. I can get my license and fly for you. You'll have your second plane done, right? And you'll need another pilot. You can train me."

"I'm not allowed to pay you until you have a commercial license and you can't get that until you're eighteen and have logged hundreds of hours."

"I know. I'll fly for you for free and I'll get my hours that way. It will save us both a ton of money. It's perfect. You need me. You won't have to pay your pilot and I won't have to pay for flight time. Whether or not you hire me after I get my commercial is entirely up to you."

"Who *I* hire is up to me? That's very generous of you." Claire laughed. "Hmm…"

Jill set to scrubbing bugs off the nose of the plane. "You say expansion is the only way your company can become really profitable and I can help. It's better than hiring some stranger off the street."

"I can't trust just anyone. If I train someone in my business, they can take away all my work. Pilots will cut your throat for a job. That's why I can't hire anyone around here. They might steal my business."

Jill set her brows to skeptical. "I get it: 'Survivor' in the sky. I'll give you immunity."

"It's hard," Claire said. "Why anyone would want to become a pilot nowadays, I don't know."

"Yeah, right," Jill said. "All that freedom. A life in the skies. Unlimited horizons." Her heart was really starting to bleed for her. Not.

"Trustworthy is the most import aspect of a hired pilot. If I can't rely on you, there's nothing."

"Who's more trustworthy than someone who learned the hard way what happens if you screw up?" Jill plugged the static port while she scrubbed around it. "I'll qualify for a commercial license the second I turn eighteen. Our business will be booming by then."

"Our?" Claire asked. "You're going to help me pay gas, taxes, inspections, engine overhauls, insurance and all the other expenses?"

Jill tried to think of a new approach. She scrubbed the struts until she thought of one. "Don't you think you better teach me to fly? I mean, I'm not going to quit. I'll never quit. Isn't it better that you make sure I'm a good pilot? In fact, you could say it's your humanitarian duty, a mercy to the world. Someone has to teach me how to fly properly before I hurt someone else."

"You and your humanitarian duties," Claire laughed. "You do

have a point." She picked up the hose and sprayed off the plane.

Jill stood next to her with pleading eyes.

Claire took a deep breath. "You'll wash the plane?" Claire's eyes were sparkling, like hope was returning to them. Jill knew she was thinking about what she said, about hiring her as a pilot for her business.

"Every week." Jill held out her hand to shake on the deal.

Claire threw the hose down. "And if I give you a second chance, how do I know you won't get impatient again and pull a bonehead move?"

Jill broke into a smile. "You have to have faith."

41 Final Approach

Prom was nothing. Nothing compared to what Jill had coming up. Prom didn't have much potential to kill her like the day she would solo. At least, she was on the ground where no nasty winds could overpower her. She could handle this, she thought as she looked at her ice-blue shimmery platforms. In order to calm down, she told herself that it was *only* prom.

As she stood by Claire's plane in her morning-sky-blue satin prom dress with little spaghetti straps that criss-crossed on her bare back, she shivered with excitement. She tried to keep warm by keeping her feet dancing as she waited. When he did finally call her, Robbie had told her to meet him at the Charlie row of hangars. She had no idea why — other than Robbie thought limos were a yawn. Too bad they couldn't go to prom in a plane.

It was getting dark and Nikka had already called from the limo right after Cesar had picked her up. Jill wished she was in the limo with them but whatever Robbie had planned was going to be fun too. She was glad she had convinced Mom to drop her off and not wait around to take pictures. She promised they would drop by home on the way to dinner. Mom wanted photos to put in an album next to her own. In Mom's book, prom was important enough to end Jill's grounding. Jill imagined Mom's prom must have been something as regal as Prince Charming's ball, making her feel like Cinderella. Jill hoped Robbie would just show up soon.

Fidgeting nervously with her hair, she accidentally pulled a lock out of the up-do. Mom had curled her hair in long ringlets and gathered a little at the crown of her head. Jill had to admit that she looked elegant and pretty. Robbie would probably keel over when he saw her — that is if he ever arrived.

After ten more minutes of waiting, Jill started to wonder if she was being stood up. That would explain a lot. Maybe Robbie had planned this all along — to get back at her. It was rotten — making her think she was going to prom and getting all dressed up in this stupid dress, standing here like a fool.

He had been so short on the phone. Practically, the only thing he said was meet him at the airport at six. As rushed and abrupt as he sounded, she thought he was just in a hurry but now she thought otherwise.

The text messages he had been sending all week were no help. They were cryptic — something about Nat Rader joining the Falcons, exclamation point. And other sports statistics that she had no idea what he was talking about. As if she was one of the boys. Maybe Robbie thought of her that way and as nothing more. Jill started to feel her hopes sink. Who knew what he was thinking? She pulled out her cell and texted him "Where are you?" even though Mom would lecture her about going over the plan's limit. In some ways, it was unfortunate that Mom was back in action. Not many though, because it was a huge relief.

She decided to stand there being an idiot for five more minutes and then get out of there before anyone saw her alone. Where was Robbie?

She listened to music in the distance as she berated herself for being stupid enough to believe Robbie had really wanted to date her. Clearly, he was having his revenge by ditching her. That's why he had told her to go to the airport: to make her look like a doofus standing around in an evening gown at a place she had to show her face again. A face trying to earn the respect of other pilots. She had only just restarted her flight lessons recently. She had a lot to live down at the airport. Walking around in a prom dress wouldn't make it any easier. She was trying to show everyone she was serious, not frivolous.

The music ramped up. It was coming from someone's hangar. Jill decided she wouldn't wait another minute. Every second longer she risked being seen by someone passing by. She started walking toward the back gate. She'd have to walk home and going out the back gate was longer but hopefully no one would see her in this ridiculous dress.

As she passed the corner, she heard the music get louder — it was coming from the Delta row, the row she would have to pass to get to the gate. Suddenly, the CAP hangar door slid open.

Jumping, Jill hid behind the end wall of the hangar row. She heard footsteps coming. Darn, people were at the CAP hangar. She was going to be seen by a classmate, no doubt. She looked for someplace to hide but there was only a fire hydrant nearby. Suddenly, Trevor came around the corner so fast, he ran into Jill.

"I'm sorry," Trevor said gripping Jill's arm to make sure she didn't fall over from the impact of him ramming into her. "What are you doing here?"

Ummmm. Waiting like a loser for a fake date. She didn't say anything.

"We're having a party in the CAP hangar. You should come."

It was nice of Trevor but she couldn't show her face at a pre-prom party. Not only because she would be the only one without a date but also because of the humiliation from people who knew she had said she was going to prom with Robbie. "No, I can't. I was just about to go for a flight."

"Like that?" He pointed to her dress.

"You don't like my flight suit?" She flounced the silky skirt.

"It's hot, but I've never seen anyone fly in a dress before."

Was he flirting? He called her hot. But she still couldn't go to the party.

He continued. "You have to come for my Death Defyers project. Come see."

Jill didn't know what project he was talking about and she didn't want to find out. She had to make her escape before anyone else saw her. "I have to go." With a little wave, she quickly turned back to head for the gate and ran smack into Robbie.

"Wha?" she said.

"You aren't going to the party?" Robbie's eyes were amused. "Guess we'll just have to bring the party to you."

Trevor whistled and a dozen people poured out of the CAP hangar toward her. Neil, Coby, Heath and their dates rushed down the row.

"What's going on?" Jill asked.

"The reason I wanted you to meet me here," Robbie said, leading her down the Delta row, "is because we're going to take our prom pictures near the new CAP trainer." He motioned to the CAP hangar. Jill saw a plane inside. It was a beat-up but beautiful Cessna

182, four-seater, single-engine, high-wing.

"You guys got a plane?!"

"Oh yeah," Robbie beamed. "Isn't she a thing of beauty? Come look." He took her arm and directed her to the hangar. Jill noticed he looked mighty fine in his dark suit with a white silk shirt, but more than that she felt the warmth of his side as he guided her to the Cessna. "Old Vern left it to us in his will. His estate just settled. He gave us a plane!"

Jill gazed at the plane incredulously. That was a really wonderful thing Old Vern did. Jill suddenly felt honored she had been with Old Vern during his passing. And now his flying legacy would bring many more to the sky he loved.

After admiring the plane, Lieutenant Barry hand-towed it out of the hangar to set it up for photos, with the runway in the background. As everyone else gathered around the Cessna, Robbie didn't leave the hangar. He retrieved something from a back table. It was a white rose corsage. He slipped it on Jill's arm. She smiled widely. It hit her that Robbie was there. Her date. Smiling back at her. His eyes were so warm and genuine. However confusing the last two weeks had been, his welcoming demeanor was unmistakable now.

She wanted to ask him why he had barely talked to her, but he took her hand and led her out to the crowded plane.

"You look beautiful," he said softly and squeezed her hand.

She didn't try to speak. She smiled as a response instead.

As they greeted everyone, he held her hand. It was weird that she felt so comfortable, so natural, with a guy she barely knew, but holding his hand felt so right, so perfect.

A black sedan came around the corner. It was a limo. Lieutenant Barry snapped pictures as three couples piled out of the limo, including Nikka and Cesar.

Nikka looked like a hippie at her hand-fasting ceremony. Her long, flowing skirt in sun-bleached, dingy white (beige) nicely accented her silk and lace camisole bodice. Garlands of white quartz and moonstones hung from her neck and she wore big silver and onyx rings on her hands. She certainly could win most original outfit tonight, but she looked beautiful in her own style. Caesar wore an eighteenth century, high-collared shirt with voluminous sleeves and pants in a matching chestnut hue.

"You're here," Jill exclaimed when Nikka rushed her.

"I'm ready to boogie," Nikka said. "Let's get these pictures over with." Nikka draped her arm around the nose of the plane and leaned against it. "Did you hear why we're doing this?"

Jill looked at Robbie, who was trying to wipe grease off the bottom cowling. He looked up at her. "Trevor's film," he said.

Trevor was looping around the plane filming every angle with his digicam. When he got to the front, he trained his lens on Jill. "So, tell us FlyGirl: what was it like to be the only girl in the history of our school to fly a plane and survive a crash — without a license I might add."

Jill's happiness declared a May Day, plummeting to the bottom of her stomach. So there it was. Death Defyers. She was the Death Defyer. He was recording her idiot move in some project. She wanted to run and hide.

"He's gonna post this segment on our video yearbook, so watch what you say," Robbie teased. "We'll be able to look back on this year forever."

As Trevor spoke a segue into the camera, Jill stepped under the wing trying to evade him. But he followed her. "You think surviving prom night is something," he held the camera on himself as he spoke, "then check out this chick. She survived an airplane crash." He turned the camera toward her. "Tell us how you managed to get out alive? Did you know how to land?"

Jill thought she better say something and then maybe Trevor would back off. "No, but I do now. I've been taking lessons." She opened the door on the pilot's side. "Do you know what these things do?" She motioned to the instruments.

Robbie, Nikka and Cesar were watching them. Trevor came around the strut and squeezed in the door jamb with Jill, filming the cockpit. She pointed to the attitude gyro. "This one tells you if you're going up or down or turning. Very important if you ever go in the clouds."

After Trevor finished filming her explanation of every instrument, she looked up and saw Nikka and Cesar dancing around each other.

Jill pulled Trevor away from the plane and pointed to Nikka's outfit.

"Check out Nikka's digs."

Trevor focused the digicam on Nikka's shoes.

"Cruelty-free woven hemp in natural beige," Nikka said as she pointed her toes, modeling her shoes.

"The color of dirt," Trevor said. "How convenient."

"That's me. Practical to a fault."

"But beautiful just the same," Jill said and hugged her. She was so glad her bestfriend was there and especially glad Trevor had moved on. He was now setting the digicam on a tripod in front of the plane.

All the couples lined up next to the plane for a group picture. As Jill stood next to Robbie in her simple, elegant gown, she held his hand and grinned. The warmth of his hand chased all her cares away. With the cameras capturing the moment, she tried not to smile too big. If her smile could have reflected how she felt, it would have stretched out of range anyway.

Several cars pulled up to the fence. Decked-out seniors hollered out the windows of their vehicles. Some cute prom-going guy yelled at Jill. "Hey, FlyGirl, take me for a ride."

Robbie leaned in to whisper in Jill's ear, "Yep, I have the coolest girlfriend in school." He kissed her cheek. Jill didn't know whether to be more excited by Robbie's kiss or the label he gave her. Girlfriend.

Suddenly, dozens of cars parked next to the fence and honked. It looked like the whole senior class was having a pre-party on the airfield. They rushed the gate and gathered around the plane. Music blared out the booming speakers in the hangar, and Nikka and Caesar danced like they were on TV, jumping up to use the limo hood as a stage until the driver shooed them off.

Lieutenant Barry tried to keep everyone from pulling on the ailerons and wagging the rudder of the plane. Chelsea showed up with her date and touched the knife-edge of the prop carefully, like she was inspecting it for nicks.

"Hi," Chelsea said to Jill. "Before CAP yesterday, we saw you land. Is it hard?"

Jill nodded. "It takes practice."

More people asked questions of the student pilot. As she fielded them through several songs, she noticed Robbie looking at her like he wanted to pull her away from the crowd. There was definitely something on his mind. She hoped it was an explanation of why he hadn't called her all week except for his brief instructions to meet him at the airport.

When almost everyone finally left for dinner, Nikka gathered Robbie and Jill next to the plane. "One more." Nikka held up her camera. "Just the two of you."

Jill and Robbie posed in front of the prop. She felt like the luckiest girl alive to be there with her friends. With exaggerated fanfare, Trevor turned his digicam on them. Robbie took Jill's hand and faced her. Nikka, Cesar, Trevor and his date circled around them. Two couples were in the limo but the doors were closed and the windows were completely opaque.

"Drum roll, please," Trevor yelled from behind the lens.

"What's going on?" Jill asked.

Turning red, Robbie reached in his pocket. "Jill, I want you to have something to remember how I feel about you. Moving three states away isn't going to change that. When you wear this," he handed her a box, "I want you to think about us."

She opened the box. Inside was a small sterling silver airplane. Jill turned red and buried her face in Robbie's neck. He put the necklace on her.

"Wild," Trevor sang, "wild horsepower couldn't drive me away."

"Shut up, man," Robbie said, but he was obviously relieved at the break in tension.

Trevor stepped in for a close-up shot of their faces, scarlet with emotion. Robbie gently pushed the camera away.

Lieutenant Barry interrupted, "You ready?" he asked Trevor and climbed in the plane.

"Yep," Trevor said and turned to Jill to explain, "We're getting an overhead shot of prom for the video. There's two more seats available." He motioned to the back of the plane as he hopped in.

"Hold on," Robbie told Trevor and then whispered in Jill's ear, "I told you I had something special planned for prom."

"Thanks for the necklace. I love it." She touched the plane that was hanging near her heart. "But why didn't you call me all week? I didn't know what was going on."

"Sorry. I had some things I had to do," he smiled sheepishly. "I got into the Air Force Academy. I have a shot at being a fighter pilot!"

"No way," Jill said.

"What'd you think I was in CAP for? It helps you get into the Academy."

"That's awesome." She hugged him.

"I had to get some things off before the deadline. I was behind because my application was dead in the water after the crash. It's been non-stop all week, and it's not over yet. But I'm here now." He smiled warmly. He leaned in. She met his kiss. Her head spun more than banking sixty degrees — the rush was so intense. Intoxicating as it was, she had to know what he meant about moving three states away and "us."

"When do you leave for the Academy?" she asked.

"Three weeks."

"That's so soon."

"I know, but I was thinking you could visit me. You have to fly cross-country to get your commercial license, right? A hundred-mile flight is required."

Trevor hollered out the plane, "You two coming? Let's go to prom," he joked.

Robbie waved for him to wait a minute.

"Maybe I could stop by," Jill said coyly. Everything was happening so fast. Robbie himself was fast. He'd be perfect for fighter jets. As speedy as he was moving tonight, something felt right about it. Wherever their airways led, she hoped they would connect in the future. They had tonight for sure. "You'll make an awesome fighter pilot."

"The odds are very small I'll make it that far. Half of those who make it into the flying program drop out, but at least I have a chance."

Jill looked at his flawless face and felt like her heart was going to burst. He kissed her long and soft, and for one perfect moment, she had everything. Love and dreams. She aimed high and now she was dancing in the stars.

42 Flight Plan

For ground school, Jill watched videos online and Claire filled in the rest, grilling her until she was able to pass the written and oral exams. With all the maneuvers down and a head full of aerodynamics, rules of the sky and about a million more things, Jill was ready for her solo. A payment plan took care of her penalty with the FAA — paid off in only forty months. She didn't care as long as she could fly. And fly she did. With school out, she was able to get two or three flights in a day, even with the distraction of looking at her prom photos over and over again. What a magical night. Robbie called when he could, but he had many deadlines to get out of the way first. Their first non-prom date would be Saturday night, after her solo. Her head was spinning.

With only twenty-four hours until her big moment, her solo, she was all nerves. She biked to the airport faster than ever before, but the release of energy didn't help. Tripping as she got off her bike, she fell against the hangar wall. Inside, she found Jack mounting the magnetic compass in the homebuilt plane. Sitting in the front seat, he set a screwdriver to the instrument panel. There were two tandem seats installed.

"It's a fast bugger," Jack said.

"Do you think she'll ever let me fly it when I'm a pilot?" Jill touched its plexiglass canopy.

"Sure. It's nice to be around someone inspired by her dream." He searched for more screws in a small paper bag. "Sounds like you have a place in her business. I know she's hoping you can work with her. After you get your commercial license?"

"Hold up." Jill controlled a shake. She woke up this morning a little trembly. "I haven't even soloed yet. One step at a time. If I don't die tomorrow… Course, the not dying part is the hard part. I don't know how much luck a person gets and I've already used up a lot."

Jack looked up at her. "And how are you feeling?"

"Scared to death."

"You?" He climbed out of the plane and Jill climbed in.

"Sometimes it sucks to be driven by a dream. Sometimes I feel like it chose me, and it won't let me go. Having a dream is sort of like being stalked by a serial killer on steroids."

Jack watched her play with the stick, like an aerobatics show pilot looping and spinning, her head falling against the head rest and flopping forward. His eyes glimmered as he watched her. "Doll, you were meant for this. You'll hit it tomorrow. Don't you worry."

Jill climbed out of the plane. "I think I can. I think I can."

Jack looked down at the rag in his hand. "You know, Jill, I'm always here for you..." He picked up an engine part. "In case you need a new carburetor... or compass..."

Jill smiled and hugged him. "I know. Thanks. You'll be there tomorrow?"

"Wouldn't miss it." He sat on a stool and looked out in the distance. "I remember when Claire was about to solo. Everything changes after the solo. It's a rite of passage that really has no comparison. Being up in the sky alone. You're brave to want to do that."

"Brave or crazy?" Jill smiled.

"Both. You won't catch me up there alone. Hell no." Jack chuckled and returned to his work.

Jill left to find a bucket, sponge and the dirty airplane she had a date with.

43 Microburst

It was kind of a bummer to have to wash Mr. Frib's new plane the day before her solo, but she had studied her eyes out. She couldn't drill herself one more time about the emergency procedures. She needed to be outside anyway to try to relax.

"How's the indentured servitude going?" Nikka's voice interrupted Jill's musings.

"I can't believe my eyes," Jill said. "What brings you out here? I thought you were worried about the air quality at airports," she teased.

"Just wanted to know where to go tomorrow. The lobby, right? Or can I watch from the flightline?"

"You can watch from the flightline, unless you want to go with me."

"I think solo means solo-tude-ness. You have to go it alone."

Jill picked a huge wasp off the window before scrubbing it. "These things are a pain to wash. No wonder they pay two hundred dollars a pop — to non-slaves that is. Wanna help me? Claire's plane is next. Jeez, if I had known a couple little flights would cost me weekends for the next decade, I might have headed for Mexico."

Nikka picked up a sponge. "How'd your lesson go?"

"Good. I have a prob, though."

"Yuck, what's this?" Nikka rubbed at the thick, sticky black gunk on the underside of the plane.

"Smog. You should be glad we're up there flying around collecting the smog on the belly of the bird."

"Yeah, right. Airplanes make the most smog."

Jill changed the subject quickly. "Did you win last night?"

"You know it. First place. We're trying to get on the TV dance shows. If you get on just one of those, the exposure is so good, you can get a music video gig."

"Cool. But if you get that you'll move away. Who's going to keep me out of trouble?"

"I'll visit, if you pick me up."

"You'll fly in one of these polluters?" Jill asked.

"They make planes that run on french fry grease. You could get one of those after you're an airline pilot. Captains make bank."

"I'm not sure I can get that job. Even though my criminal record will be expunged after probation, my FAA record will never be."

"So what will you do?"

"Any flying job I can get. Who cares as long as I'm up in the sky? That's the whole point, remember?"

A plane buzzed overhead. Nikka watched it disappear behind the buildings. "I can't believe tomorrow's the day. Are you ready to do that?" She motioned to the plane.

"I think so."

"You can land all by yourself now? Like in one piece? Aren't you scared? You'll be on your own. If you can't handle it, it's all over, right?"

"Is this my pep talk? Cuz it's not working." Jill turned on the hose and sprayed the soap off. "Of course, I'm totally scared. It's just me and my training now. No one else. I've already had a lot of luck. Maybe my luck's run out. How do you know?"

Nikka made an uncertain face.

"Aren't you going to say anything?" Jill asked.

"Good luck?" She said it like a question.

"Robbie can't come. He has to go to a meeting, something to do with the Academy. But you'll be on time, right? On, only, the most important day of my life?"

"Okay. I guess," Nikka teased.

"I don't want you to miss a second. Bring a video camera in case I crash. You can sell the footage."

"Wicked. Yeah, 'here's the video of my bestfriend crashing and dying.'" Nikka held out her hand miming the action. "'Pay me now.' I'm so sure."

"Works for me," Jill laughed. "And don't worry about the Townsend curse. I have a repellant." Jill pulled out the dragonfly charm from her pocket.

"Girl," Nikka patted her arm for emphasis, "more than believing in the Townsend curse, I believe in you." Nikka smiled.

Jill was beginning to feel like she believed in herself too. She sprayed off the tail, being careful to avoid splattering Nikka. Not.

44 Aim High and Fly Solo

The day of truth had come. Jill woke and immediately sat up. Today she would prove herself worthy of becoming a full-fledged pilot, if she survived her first flight alone. It was within her grasp. Almost...

"Dad, I'm gonna do it." She took a moment to lose herself in the blueness of her room. Such a warm and safe place... What if she just never left her bedroom again? It was so lovely. So solid. So ... on the ground. She dressed in her bluest jeans and shirt and stuffed her dragonfly charm in her pocket.

In the kitchen, she grabbed a Power Bar and water — she always had survival food on her now — as Mom brushed Bre's hair. Kelly sung loudly from the bathtub, her serenade making it all the way across the house.

"You ready for today?" Mom asked.

"Of course, I'm ready." Jill put a To-Go jar of Dad's ashes in her flight bag along with her aerial maps. Dad was coming with her today.

"What's today?" Bre asked.

"My first flight all alone." She hugged Bre and kissed her head. "After this, only a few more hours soloing to get my license. Taking the test for my license isn't as hard as what I'm going to do today." She wasn't really explaining this to baby Bre. She was kind of psyching herself out. She let out a sigh. "Even during the test, you aren't alone. The examiner's there if you have an emergency. Pilot In Command means there ain't no one leading the way but you. You decide everything." Bre looked up at her solemnly then ran and jumped on her Do-do bird, lost in her own, happy world.

"Jill," Mom cornered her, "You don't have to do this. If you don't feel ready... You can back out."

"I'll be fine." Jill had to escape, rushing to the door. Mom wasn't helping her confidence.

"Be careful," Mom called after her. "I love you."

On the way to the airport, Jill's heart pumped so fast, she thought she might pass out. She tried to keep her mind on the task, not the fear, today held. But what if she couldn't do it? She would be all alone up there. She couldn't decide to back out later.

* * *

Claire took Jill to breakfast at a cozy diner near the airport. She said she had something to give her.

Sitting in the booth, Jill's leg shook in nervousness. "What if I forget to set the altimeter? What if a wind shear slams me into a mountain? What if I freeze? What if something comes up that I can't handle? What'll I do—"

Claire sipped her coffee. "I remember how scary it was. But you'll get through it. Many have." She doused her pancakes in syrup. "All those who have gone before you."

"What?" Jill devoured her eggs.

"I don't know. I suddenly felt... connected. Like I belong here. Like I'm a part of everything and everyone."

Jill frowned. "I'm going to fly a plane and land successfully all by myself for the first time today and you're talking about how you feel?" Jill teased.

"We all go through the same things — testing ourselves. Whether or not we cut the mustard is all how we decide to see ourselves. Jill, even in your solo flight, you won't be alone. You have all those who have gone before you. Trust yourself."

"But then I worry that I can't make myself think the right thoughts to succeed, you know?"

"Practice." Claire smirked.

"Practice. Practice. Practice." Jill downed her second glass of orange juice. "So, what did you want to give me?"

"Huh?" Claire chugged the last of her coffee.

"You said you wanted to give me something at breakfast."

"I just did. All my wisdom — Priceless." Claire stole a piece of bacon from her.

"Thirty-something years and that's all you got?" Jill laughed. "I'm in trouble."

* * *

At the airport, Edmond, in his Lakers cap, and Burtie were sitting in their lawn chairs with a view of the runway. They waved enthusiastically as Jill climbed in Claire's Cessna 150. She turned on the radios and listened to the traffic. It was a busy day. She switched them back off as she waited for Claire to finish signing her logbook, giving her the endorsement she needed to solo. Jill fidgeted with her headset. Her hands were up to their old shaking tricks. She tried to calm herself with deep, slow breaths, just like Tia and Nikka had taught her.

Claire closed her logbook and stuck it in the seat next to Jill. "You ready?"

How did she know if she was ready for this? How does anyone ever know? Jill could tell from the look in Claire's eyes that Claire could see her shaking. Jill willed her hands to hold the yoke steady, but her feet nearly bounced off the rudder pedals they were jerking so hard. "Ready as I'll ever be." She just wanted to get it over with now. It was going to be such a relief to have her first solo flight behind her.

Jill had to look away from Claire's eyes. She could read Claire's thoughts: she was wondering if she was sending her student off to die. She was probably a little scared too.

"Remember what I told you about your radio announcements today?" Claire asked.

Jill nodded.

"You'll do fine. Whatever happens, fly the airplane, fly the airplane, fly the airplane. You'll keep your head. I believe in you."

"Thanks." Jill felt a little weight lift off her.

"I'll be right here." Claire shut the door and moved away from the plane. Jill started it up and listened to the lively airfield.

"Big Bear Traffic," Jill addressed the other pilots in the area, "Cessna Two Five Whiskey, taxiing to the run-up area for student solo."

"For student solo" was what Claire had told her to announce so everyone would give her a little more breathing room. Everyone would understand the nervousness of this rite of passage and clear the way.

"Good luck, Cessna Two Five Whiskey," a voice said over the radio.

Another announced he was on downwind and added, "Good luck to the pilot soloing."

A few more voices clamored on the radio and Jill thought she might cry. It really was a community and she was about to join them.

She could feel them rooting for her. Pilots were an awesome group to belong to. After a few more "good lucks" and "you can do its," she told herself to concentrate. "Get your head in the game," Jill said out loud.

At the edge of the runway, Jill glanced at the empty copilot seat next to her. It was a frightening sight to see. She missed her instructor already, but she had trained for this. She was ready. This was it. This was the moment she had been waiting for.

Oh, but what if she got in a jam? Terror overtook her again, stifling the air out of her lungs as bad thoughts screamed in her head over and over. What if she suddenly forgot all that she had been taught? What if a huge crosswind came up on takeoff and threw the airplane into a building? Fog could roll in and hide the nearby range. She methodically forced these thoughts out of her mind, replacing them with the excitement of becoming a pilot. She took the dragonfly charm out of her pocket and kissed it for good luck. Although, as she put her hands on the controls, she knew, today, fate was in her own hands, and kissing the dragonfly was just a symbol to herself.

As she scanned the instruments and watched the rising oil pressure and temperature, she calmed herself. "You can do this." She shook out her sweaty palms.

After checking the sky, she turned the plane onto the runway and powered up. Gas rich, trim set, flaps up. Her feet guided the plane steady down the centerline. The engine roared and the plane shook. As soon as she was going fast enough, she pulled back on the yoke and the plane lifted into the air. When she had enough altitude, she turned the plane to circle the town.

To calm her nerves, she bobbed her ponytail to the music in her head, singing the silly song she had been singing to her sisters. "Aim high, cuz if you aim low, that's probably where you'll go. Aim high." It made her laugh, releasing some tension. She was glad she was alone so no one could hear her.

Soaring in the solitude of endless sky, Jill remembered her first landing, the crash. She forced herself to think about all the training landings in-between that crazy day and today. She couldn't afford to be afraid of landing this thing now. "Come on, Jill," she yelled at herself, "You can do this." She bit her lip.

Worried that Claire had booby-trapped something to test her, she checked the instrument panel again. Everything seemed normal. She looked back up and couldn't see anything but mist.

"Oops." She wasn't supposed to fly into the gossamer clouds. She didn't mean to — it snuck up. She hoped Claire on the ground couldn't see her mistake. She pushed the control wheel in, rolled to the left and blue sky greeted her again. "No biggie," Jill said to herself. She knew she had to get over her mistake quickly or she'd just make more. She flew closer to the airport. "Hope no one saw that." She looked down at the active airport. "Just the whole town."

She waved the wings for those watching on the airfield. Her whole entourage was there: Mom, her sisters, Nikka, Burtie, Edmond, Jack and Claire, taking notes. They could see for themselves that she was the sole pilot in command, of both the airplane and her life. Applying rudder, she worked with the wind, a force she couldn't control, crabbing into it. Then, she turned back toward the airport, to prove to Mom and everyone just exactly what she could control. She could handle this thing called life and it was fun. Even something as big as flying. She entered the landing pattern with a hard left and searched the sky for any company. Only one plane on final. She knew she had plenty of spacing between.

So far, so good. The hardest part, the landing, was yet to come. "Way to psyche yourself up, Jill." She thought about overshooting the runway. Sometimes overshoots were even fatal. Her first landing had proven disastrous. "Don't think about that." She needed all the pep talks she could give herself. "Focus. You're exactly where you want to be. You're doing it! I won't overshoot. I won't miss the runway. I won't blow it."

A wind shear bumped her upward. "I won't die." Up, up, up and down in a shear. "Much."

As she entered Final Approach, she saw her family and friends on the flightline, awaiting her victorious return. It was time to land already and finish meeting her destiny. She saw an aircraft taking off from the airport as she closed in. It wasn't supposed to take off with her on final, but it was fast and soon moved to a safe distance. Jill cranked the flaps down.

Flying into the wind, she angled the plane exactly in line with the numbers of the runway. A crosswind blew her to the side, but she corrected with rudder, a wing-slip low.

Managing the ground effect from the runway right below her, she powered down the airplane and missed the numbers, but that was okay — plenty of runway was left. She checked her instruments quickly and tried to take a deep breath.

The plane was floating — it really made quite a difference not having the extra weight of her instructor. Finally, half way down the runway she sunk the main wheels down. With a slight bump, she set the nose wheel down. Both feet cranked the two brakes smoothly. She slowed the plane successfully before she turned off the last exit of the runway and taxied to the tarmac near her cheering crowd.

She did it!

Jill jumped out of the plane as soon as the prop stopped. She found lots of hugs as she laughed herself silly from relief and joy. Even Claire gave her a bear hug before inspecting her plane for damage.

"Not even one dent!" Claire joked. "Way to go!"

Mom snapped photos. "My girl, a pilot. Wow," she said.

"Darn good one, too," Claire said. "Congratulations."

As her heart leapt with delight, Burtie, Edmond and Jack took turns congratulating her.

A dog tied to a fence post next to the lobby started barking enthusiastically. From behind the lobby, Robbie came bolting out. Jill didn't think she could smile any wider. Robbie rushed up to her holding yellow roses.

"Lookin' good, FlyGirl," he said. Jill gleamed as she looked into his eyes. Excitement spilled out of them, and it was so visceral and real, she felt like he was really sharing in her joy.

"You were here? You saw?" she asked.

"For the best part. The landing." He pulled her into a hug. "You did it!"

"I did it!" She wanted to kiss him.

He looked at everyone still cheering for Jill, then remembered to hand her the flowers. Nikka nodded at the gesture of flowers and said, "Smooth."

Jill wrapped herself up in his arms. He kissed her hair. "You rule," he said. "Let's celebrate."

"A victory ride up around the pattern?" Claire asked. "Who wants to go?"

Jill and Robbie shot their hands up in the air.

Robbie looked at the Cessna 150, the two seats.

"We can take the new CAP trainer," Claire said. "Lieutenant Barry's in the hangar." She headed to the CAP hangar across the airfield. The dog was still barking at the fence where it was tied.

"That's Kali." He went to get her.

Nikka danced around Jill. "You did it, girl. Just promise me you'll bring up smog control at every pilot meeting, okay?"

"For sure," Jill laughed. "There's room in the CAP Cessna. You wanna come for a ride?"

"Uh, no, my feet like the earth." She hugged Jill. Nikka started dancing around, singing as cheesily as she could, "Did you ever know that you're my hero…"

Robbie returned with Kali. "Since there's a seat open, can she come?" Robbie asked as he stooped to pet the brown Labrador.

"Maybe — if you can tell me what makes an airplane fly?" Jill teased.

Robbie looked at her as his answer, but he said, "Gas." They laughed. She turned to her sisters and asked the same as she picked Bre up and twirled her around, "What makes an airplane fly?"

"Lift! Lift!" Both Bre and Kelly had had it drilled into their heads by a sister who knew no limits. Well, maybe the stratosphere … for now.

Robbie let Kali pull him around so she could sniff around the hangars.

Mom, who was hoarding her young'uns far away from any aircraft, caught Jill before she took off. "Jill," she started and then looked down quietly.

Jill put her arm around Mom. "You okay?"

"I want to tell you something…" She looked her daughter in the eyes, letting the tears trickle. "Jill, you're my lift."

A group of dragonflies flew in and circled the airfield, a beautiful flock of flapping friends. Jill tried to reach up and touch the magical swarm, but they flew away, as quietly as they had come. Dad was a dragonfly. His time spent flying life was short but beautiful. Through his early death, he showed her that responsibility was simply responding to what calls you in life.

As they watched the dragonfly flock move across the airfield, Nikka mouthed "Wow" and squeezed Jill's hand.

When Claire pulled up to the tarmac in the Cessna 182, Jill, Robbie and Kali piled in. Jill was in the pilot's seat, of course. With Claire as co-pilot, they were ready to go in two minutes.

"How much is this gonna cost?" Jill asked as Claire finished the pre-flight checklist.

"Don't worry: I'll take it out of your pay next year," she snickered. "You got it, Pilot." Claire took her hands off the controls.

"I got it," Jill repeated as was standard operating procedure.

The 182 took off even faster than any plane Jill had been in. It grabbed the sky faster than a speeding dragonfly. The engine was louder and more powerful than anything Jill had flown. In seconds, they were over the lake. Claire took over flying for a few moments so Jill could look at the beauty beneath them. The sun sparkled spellbound on the water.

Jill turned around and laughed at Kali, whose hot breath steamed up the window she was trying to look out of. Eventually, she sat down and smiled a big slobbery smile. As Robbie pet Kali, he gazed at Jill. She could hardly stand it. The intensity of his soft eyes made her burn with electricity. She had to look away, out in front of her, before she passed out. She couldn't believe Robbie had come to her big day. She didn't know how he was able to make it but she loved having him there to share this.

Jill looked out at the bright, blue sky. The horizon seemed to stretch out forever. She whispered vespers to Dad as she tried to see the end of the sky. She opened the window and took out Dad's To-Go jar. As the wind fought her hand, she spread his ashes out the window and into the boundless sky.

There was no end to the sky, just eternity. She knew he was proud — just as she was of herself.

She was FlyGirl and not even gravity could keep her down.

A Free Ride

Still wondering what VFR means? Want to know how to get a free flight? Check out SydBlue.com for info about the Young Eagles program and other resources. Even actor Harrison Ford who served as chairman of the program for several years takes people up in his airplane just to introduce them to the wonders of flight.

At SydBlue.com:

- Test yourself and see how much you know about flying.
- Find flying schools, young aviator programs, and info to get you started.
- Learn how to become a pilot and watch what other pilots say about flying.
- Read about teen and women pilots who had to overcome all their own obstacles, like FlyGirl, to reach their goals.

Quick Quiz

How much do you already know about flight? Take this quick quiz now and check out the answers at SydBlue.com.

1.   Flaps:
      a.   are moveable extensions of the wings
      b.   increase lift and drag
      c.   are used during landing
      d.   all of the above

2. The four forces acting on a plane in straight and level flight are:
      a.   lift, pull, push and drag
      b.   lift, weight, thrust and drag
      c.   lift, centrifugal, gravity and drag
      d.   lift, inertial, gravity and weight

3. Which one of these does the airplane's foot pedals NOT control:
      a.   the rudder
      b.   steering on the ground
      c.   the wheel's brakes
      d.   the ailerons

4. Which one of these conditions causes the plane to require a longer runway for takeoff?
      a.   humidity
      b.   hot temperatures
      c.   elevation
      d.   all of the above

5. At what age can you get a license and fly by yourself in the USA?
      a.   15
      b.   16
      c.   17
      d.   18

6. Which one of these does not affect how much fuel is used up?
      a. '   weight of aircraft, baggage and passengers
      b.   visibility
      c.   airspeed
      d.   distance of the flight